CONTENTS

front cover by Matt Wagner thanks to Kevin Smith
front cover color and back cover by Mark Wheatley

EXPO INTRO SPX99

Mike Zarlenga Executive Direcector

When I think of The EXPO-SPX, I am reminded of the movie City Slickers. In the movie the characters played by Billy Crystal, Daniel Stern, and Bruno Kirby are three best friends who do everything together. At the time of the story, each is suffering their own personal versions of a mid-life crisis, and the need to get away from it all to sort out their lives. Stern and Kirby have found the perfect way to both solve their problems and sooth their souls: take Crystal on a "great outdoors" vacation to become a cowboy on an actual cattle drive. Billy Crystal finds himself discussing the "meaning of life" with Jack Palance (playing a hard-as-nails trail boss). Palance discloses to Crystal the meaning of life by holding up his index finger and saying that the meaning of life is one thing, everything else is irrelevant.

The reason The EXPO-SPX reminds me of this movie stems from my travels this summer. I have taken it upon myself to visit as many conventions as possible in an effort to improve The EXPO and make it the best show in the country. In my travels I have noticed that The EXPO does one exceptional thing. At The EXPO, we do not try to supplement the focus of our convention with retail exhibitors, action figures, movies, adult magazines, and television stars. We focus on promoting independent comic book artists, creators, and publishers by bringing them together to meet fans, retailers, and other industry professionals. Those who have attended The EXPO over the years know that in 1998 we did this better than any of our previous four years. No one doubts that 1999 promises to be the best EXPO yet. Our continued partnership with the International Comics Arts Festival will provide the same international flair that fans of The EXPO have become accustomed to. In addition our new partnership with the Professional Association of Comics Entertainment Retailers will bring in more industry professionals than ever before. The EXPO also manages to produce this annual anthology of independent comics. Each of these elements is important. And each element serves to support one exceptional thing. That one exceptional thing is to provide a showcase for independent comic artists, creators, and publishers.

So, without further adieu, I am pleased to present to you the third EXPO anthology showcasing a small portion of the vast creative talent that makes The EXPO-SPX a can't miss event. If you only have one thing scheduled, it should be The EXPO-SPX – everything else is irrelevant!

THE EXPO99 COMIC: Coordinated by Chris Oarr & Brian Clopper, produced by Mark Wheatley (Insight Studios) & Stev Conley. THE EXPO is a not-for-profit organization created to promote comics, animation, cartooning, & related popu lar art forms that celebrate the historic & ongoing contribution of comics, animation, &cartooning to art & cultur

Sponsors include **Big Planet Comics** (Bethesda, MD & Vienna, VA), **Atomic Books** (Baltimore, MD), **Beyond Comics** (Gaithersburg, MD), **Closet of Comics** (College Park, MD), **Dreaming City Comics** (Arlington, VA), **Million Year Picni** (Cambridge, MA), **St. Mark's Comics** (NYC), and **Phoenix Enterprises** (Herndon, VA).

For more information about THE EXPO, visit:
www.spxpo.com

WHEN I WAS SIXTEEN, I HAD MY FIRST REAL GIG IN A NIGHTCLUB. IT WAS FOR AN END-OF-SEASON SOCCER TEAM PARTY, AND THESE GUYS JUST ATE US UP...

THE "WORST" GIG I EVER HAD
WORDS: CHRIS STAROS
PICTURES: RICH TOMMASO
PUB
SHE WAS JUST-17!!
IT WAS THE FIRST TIME THAT WE EVER REALLY JELLED AS A BAND, & ALSO THE FIRST TIME I EVER WITNESSED A GROUP OF AMERICANS TURN INTO A BUNCH OF DRUNK, SINGING, IRISHMEN.
AND THE WAY SHE LOOKED--FUCK, YEAH!
WHEN THE GIG WAS OVER, GREG AND TOMMY, THE TWO CAPTAINS OF THE TEAM, ASKED IF WE'D LIKE TO DO AN OUTDOOR PARTY THEY WERE PLANNING TO THROW THE FOLLOWING WEEKEND.
HOW MUCH DOES IT PAY?
WE COULD DO ABOUT $350.00
SOLD!

SO, THE NEXT SATURDAY WE FOLLOWED THEM OUT TO THE GIG. AND AFTER A FOUR HOUR DRIVE (!), WE STARTED TO WONDER WHY SUCH A DESOLATE AND UNLIKELY LOCATION HAD BEEN CHOSEN.

AND THEN JUST AS WE FINISHED SETTING UP, WE HEARD THE MOST GOD-AWFUL SOUND...

I SWEAR - THERE MUST'VE BEEN A HUNDRED BIKERS THAT PULLED UP...

AND THEN - THE GANG LEADER GOT OFF HIS HARLEY BIKE AND HEADED OUR WAY...

AND WE WERE HIP TO THAT SCENE

I REALLY APPRECIATE YOU GUYS COMIN' OUT AND PLAYIN' FOR OUR ANNUAL PARTY...
YOU'RE GONNA HAVE A GOOD TIME WITH US.
WE'RE JUST GONNA HANG OUT FOR A WHILE. MAYBE YOU GUYS COULD START JAMMIN' WHEN THE SUN GOES DOWN, COOL?
C-Cool.
SO, UM, IS THIS **CHOPPER KING** REALLY YOUR BROTHER?
WOOOO!!
ABSOLUTELY.
BUT, I THOUGHT WE WERE GONNA PLAY FOR YOUR SOCCER TEAM!
DON'T SWEAT IT, MAN... THESE GUYS KNOW HOW TO ROCK!!
CRANK! CRANK!
THAT'S WHAT I'M AFRAID OF!
OOOF!
HA!
AAAAAAAAA
HA! HA! HA!

WITHIN AN HOUR THOUGH, WE FIGURED OUT THAT OUR LIVES WEREN'T IN ANY IMMEDIATE DANGER--

IN FACT, THEY EVEN INVITED US TO PLAY IN THEIR MAKESHIFT BASEBALL GAME.

WHAT COULD BE MORE AMERICAN, RIGHT?--BASEBALL, HOT DOGS & WELL... APPLEJACK...

IT LOOKED AND **TASTED** LIKE APPLE CIDER, BUT, **MAN** DID IT PACK A PUNCH. AND WITH A COUPLE BARRELS OF THE STUFF, WE FIGURED THERE WAS NO WAY THIS CROWD WAS GONNA STAY SOBER FOR LONG.

NEEDLESS TO SAY, THEY DIDN'T DISAPPOINT US...

BUT, JUST AS WE WERE STARTING TO CRANK UP THE P.A WE NOTICED EVERYONE CHEERING ON THESE TWO BIKERS WHO WERE BRINGING A WOODEN CRATE OVER TO THE FIRE... WHEN WE GOT OVER THERE, WE COULDN'T BELIEVE WHAT WE WERE SEEING. THESE GUYS HAD JUS OPENED A WHOLE CRATE FULL OF...

AND IT WASN'T BUT SECONDS LATER BEFORE SEVERAL OF THEM REACHED INTO THE CRATE, LIT THE FUSES ...

AND CHUCKED THE STICKS INTO THE DISTANT TREES.

WE COULDN'T FUCKING BELIEVE IT...

NO WONDER THESE GUYS THREW THEIR PARTIES OUT IN THE MIDDLE OF NOWHERE!

BUT, AS SOON AS THEY GOT BORED WITH THE DYNAMITE...

... THEY TURNED THEIR ATTENTION TOWARD **US** ...

AND WE SURELY WERE **NOT** GOING TO DISAPPOINT THEM!

LET'S HIT IT, BOYS!

BAOM

I GUESS THAT WITHIN AN HOUR WE HAD TAMED THE SAVAGE BEASTS, AS EVERYONE SEEMED TO BE GROOVIN' TO THE TUNES...

BUT THEN, THE STRANGEST THING HAPPENED...

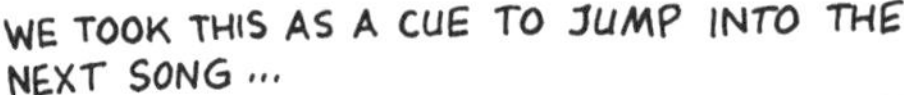

BUT, BEFORE WE KNEW WHAT WAS HAPPENING, EVERYONE TOOK OFF THE CLOTHES... AND FORMED A BIG CIRCLE AROUND US...

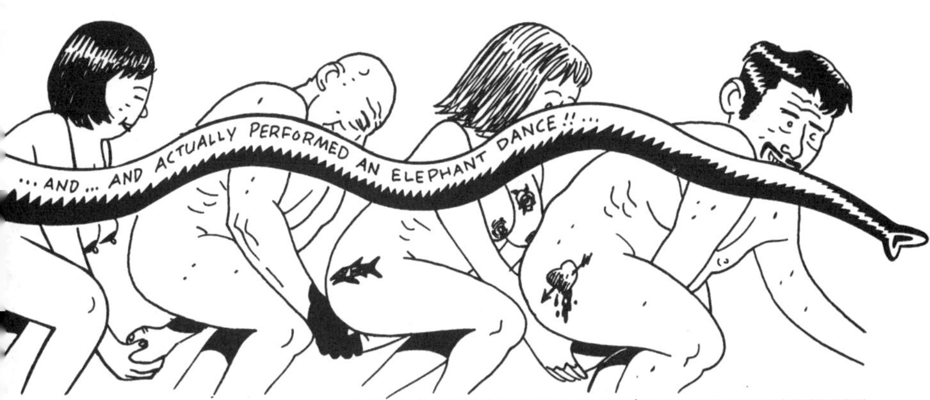

... AND ... AND ACTUALLY PERFORMED AN ELEPHANT DANCE!! ...

WE JUST LAUGHED AND STARED IN AMAZEMENT ...

AAWW... WHAM BAM THANK YOU MA'AM!!

WELL, EVENTUALLY, THE ELEPHANT DANCE ENDED AND THE SHOW CAME TO A CLOSE.

THANKS, EVERYBODY!
SEE YA NEXT YEAR!

CAN YOU BELIEVE?
NO!

MAN, NOBODY'S GONNA BELIEVE IT! -- THEY'RE JUST NOT- GET THE FUCK OUTTA HERE!

SONGS PERFORMED: 'I SAW HER STANDING THERE' © THE BEATLES
'I CAN'T GET ENOUGH OF YOUR LOVE' © BAD COMPANY AND
'SUFFRAGETTE CITY' © DAVID BOWIE.

the end

published by TOP SHELF PRODUCTIONS, INC. PO Box 1282 Marietta GA 30061-1282
INTERNET: http://www.topshelfcomix.com EMAIL: staros@bellsouth.net *or* topshelf@europa.com

the daniel witherspoon sessions

by tony consiglio

I WENT TO AN AUDITION IN NINETEEN SEVENTY TWO FOR "STAR FIGHTERS". THEY WERE CASTING FOR SEVERAL HUNDRED EXTRAS. IT LOOKED IFFY FOR A WHILE, BUT I GOT THE PART.

DUKE
GREAT YOU GOT THE PART. NEXT!

I GOT THE PART OF SNIGGEY TIK.

SNIGGEY TIK IS A KARMOPIAN AND HELPED DUKE BOX TICKLER BYPASS THE T-120 SYSTEM AND GET THE SPACE MODULATOR WORKING ON THE TWEED FIGHTER. IT WAS A PIVOTAL ROLE. IF DUKE COULDN'T FLY THE FIGHTER TO PLANET MERDE HIS COMRADES WOULD'VE BEEN DEAD FOR SURE!

IT'S THE TWENTIETH ANNIVERSARY OF STAR FIGHTERS AND MARKUSFILM IS PLANNING ON A BIG PREQUEL CALLED "THE VERY FIRST ONE".

I CALLED MARKUSFILM, TO SEE Y'KNOW, IF THEY NEED ME AGAIN BUT, THEY DECLINED TO TALK TO ME ABOUT A DEAL. THEY SAID ALL THE ALIENS WILL BE "COMPUTER GENERATED".
OH NO! TIK, WITHOUT A WORKING FLUX CAPACATOR I CAN'T GENERATE THE ONE POINT TWENTY ONE JIGGAWATTS NEEDED TO JUMP LIGHTYEARS!
COMPUTER'S CAN'T GET IN SNIGGEY TIK'S HEAD, THEY CAN'T! I AM SNIGGEY TIK!
I EVEN WENT DOWN THERE TO MARCUS FILM STUDIOS. THEY THREW ME OUT. THEY HIT ME ON MY NECK. SEE.
THANKS SNIGGEY TIK, I'LL NEVER FORGET YOU! YOU'RE A GROOVY PAL.
ONCE I CAME HOME WITH MY COSTUME ON. MY KIDS CRIED FOR DAYS. HEH. BUT AFTER A FEW WEEKS THEY GOT USED TO IT.
I'M PRETTY CLOSE WITH MY KIDS. I HAVEN'T SPOKEN TO JOEY IN YEARS. I TRY CALLING BUT HE CHANGED HIS NUMBER.
AND PETEY, WELL, HE'S BEEN IN THE STATE PEN FOR SIX YEARS NOW. I KNOW HE LOVED HIS MAMA BUT TO DIG HER DEAD BODY UP AND VIOLATE HER OVER AND OVER. ALL YOU CAN DO IS RAISE 'EM AND HOPE THEY TURN OUT RIGHT.
reenactment

MY TOTAL SCREEN TIME IN STAR FIGHTERS IS TWO MINUTES AND SIX SECONDS. THAT'S NOT SO BAD

FOUR SECONDS OF THOSE TWO MINUTES WERE SEEN IN THE THE THIRD INSTALLMENT OF STAR FIGHTERS.

THEY JUST USED STOCK FOOTAGE OF ME THEY CUT OUT FROM THE FIRST FILM.

I SHOULD'VE PROBABLY BEEN PAID FOR THAT EXTRA STUFF. I NEVER GOT PAID.

THANKS SNIGGEY TIK, I'LL NEVER FORGET YOU! YOU'RE A GROOVY PAL.

I'VE BEEN THE HEAD MANAGER OF THE CUPCAKE DIVISION AT THE SWEETIE PIE BAKERY FOR FOURTEEN YEARS NOW.
I LOVE IT THERE.

PEOPLE ASK "WHY DID YOU LEAVE ACTING TO MAKE CUPCAKES?"

I SAY, "THE REAL DOUGH IS IN BAKED GOODS!" HANH? GET IT? HA HA
HA HA HA

ACTUALLY, WE INVITED BACK EVERYONE THAT WAS IN THE ORIGINAL MOVIES.
THEY WERE GOING TO HAVE CAMEOS AND BE PAID SCALE.
MARKUSFILM

DOUBLE CROSS! 60-13 68th Road, Ridgewood, NY 11385 PHONE: 718-497-3722
INTERNET: http://members.aol.com/minitony/ EMAIL: tcdoublecross@bhotmail.com

"THE LOW-DOWN, STINKING CHEATER"
a clan Apis story
BY JAY HOSLER
C'MON, BABY.
I LOVE YOU.
LET'S GO STEADY.
DISGUSTING.
WELL, I'M SORRY, BUT THE ONLY WAY I CAN GET YOUR NECTAR IS TO STICK MY PROBOSCIS INTO YOUR NECTARIES AND SUCK IT UP.
NOT *THAT*.
ARE YOU HAPPY WITH OUR RELATIONSHIP, NYUKI?
HMM?

IT'S EQUITABLE, ISN'T IT? I GIVE YOU NECTAR AND POLLEN AND YOU SPREAD MY POLLEN TO OTHER FLOWERS.
SURE. I GET FOOD FOR THE HIVE AND YOU GET TO REPRODUCE.
WHAT'S THIS ALL ABOUT, BLOOMINGTON?
OH, IT'S THAT ORCHID OVER THERE. SHE MAKES ME SO MAD.
YEAH I SAW THAT EARLIER. WHAT IS THAT GOOFY WASP DOING?
HE'S TRYING TO MATE.
WITH AN *ORCHID?*
THIS I GOTTA SEE.
THE WASP DOESN'T KNOW IT'S AN ORCHID. HE THINKS IT'S A FEMALE WASP OF HIS SPECIES.
THAT ORCHID IS A LOW-DOWN STINKIN' CHEATER WHO DOESN'T REWARD HER POLLINATOR.
ARE YOU *SURE?*
THAT WASP SEEMS PRETTY ***ENTHUSIASTIC*** FOR SOMEONE WHO'S GETTING RIPPED-OFF.

TRUST ME, NYUKI, THAT ORCHID IS A PARASITE. IT PREYS ON THE WASP'S IMPULSE TO MATE BY RELEASING A PERFUME THAT MIMICS THE FEMALE WASP'S MATING PHEROMONE.
HELLO THERE.

TO COMPLEMENT ITS TRICKY SMELL, THE ORCHID ALSO HAS A PETAL THAT LOOKS JUST LIKE A FEMALE WASP. ATTRACTED BY THE SMELL, THE MALE WASP TRIES TO MATE WITH THE "WASP" PETAL.
LET'S GO STEADY.

AS HE DOES, THE ORCHID'S POLLEN PACKS GET STUCK TO HIS HEAD.
GAH!

EVENTUALLY, HE GIVES UP AND LEAVES, TAKING THE POLLEN WITH HIM WITHOUT RECEIVING ANY NECTAR OR USEABLE POLLEN.
SNIFF! IT'S JUST A DUMB FLOWER.

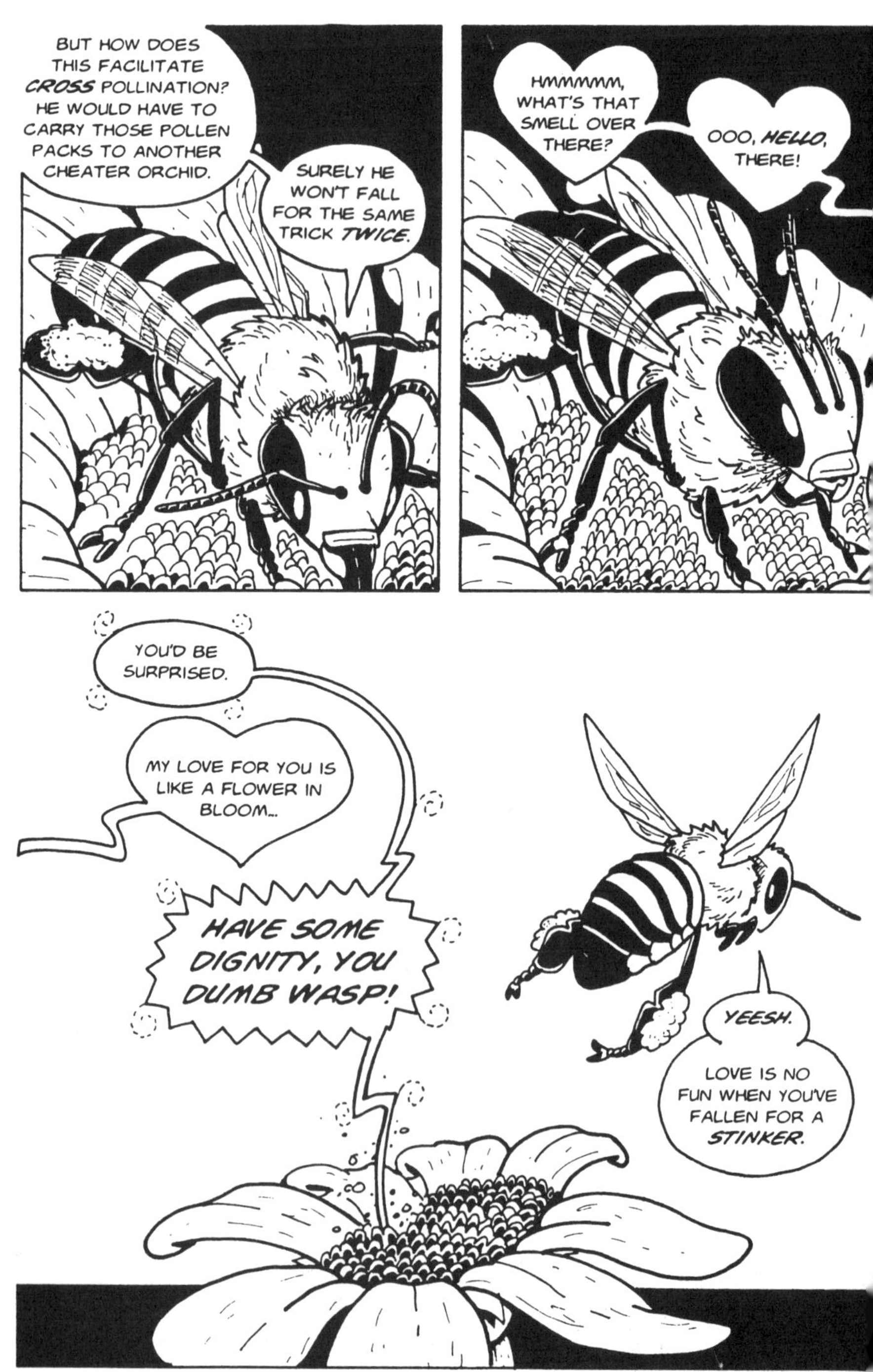
BUT HOW DOES THIS FACILITATE CROSS POLLINATION? HE WOULD HAVE TO CARRY THOSE POLLEN PACKS TO ANOTHER CHEATER ORCHID.
SURELY HE WON'T FALL FOR THE SAME TRICK TWICE.
HMMMMM, WHAT'S THAT SMELL OVER THERE?
OOO, HELLO, THERE!
YOU'D BE SURPRISED.
MY LOVE FOR YOU IS LIKE A FLOWER IN BLOOM...
HAVE SOME DIGNITY, YOU DUMB WASP!
YEESH.
LOVE IS NO FUN WHEN YOU'VE FALLEN FOR A STINKER.

JOAN REIDY 1995
"BOYS."
1997 RON REGÉ
HE ASKED IF HE COULD KISS ME
HE WAS CUTE
I WAS BORED
Sure.
I said.

T.R-'95
RR-'97
All of a sudden...
!
I realised we were kissing...
His tounge was in my mouth...
but I don't know how it got there.
?

Reidy—1995
Boys
1997—Regé
His lips were warm and soft.
It was a nice kiss
-- I guess-
I wasn't into it.
?

J. REIDY '95
BOYS
R. REGE '98
He tried...
to get me DRUNK
and SEDUCE me.
but he wasn't counting on me...
PUSH!
having a higher tolerence than him.
PLOP!

RIPPED FROM THE VERY RARE PAGES OF SILLY DADDY #19, IT'S TIME TO...

MEET THE MOTORBERRY BRANCH OF THE BERRY BRIGADE*

* If you can name all 3 of the above pictured cartoonists... you've been reading too many comics, friend! ©1999 Chiappetta

 2209 Northgate, North Riverside, IL 60546 708-447-3437
INTERNET: www.wraithspace.com/silldaddy EMAIL: sillydaddy@wraithspace.com

Maria & Magic Boy Team Up™
BY JOE CHIAPPETTA • JAMES KOCHALKA • MATT FEAZEL • & SHANE SIMMONS © 19
JC
check it out
?
JK
RAR!
YEEK!
MF
Snif Snorf
Why am I so lost?
JK
You need to love God.
JC

HIS NAME IS IG.
LETHAL CONFLICT IS WHAT HE DOES BEST.
BOLD RECONFIGURING OF BODY PARTS IS HIS MASTERFUL SPECIALITY.
HE ENCOUNTERS STEAMY ENTRAILS AND BLOODY FRESH ORGANS EVERY DAY.
HE IS NOT A DOCTOR.
LATELY, DOC, I JUST CAN'T SEEM TO MAKE SENSE OF IT ALL. HOW DID I WIND UP HERE?
ALTHOUGH, RIGHT NOW, HE'S SEEING ONE.

HENCHMEN THERAPY

ter/penciller/letterer **BRIAN CLOPPER** inker **TED TUCKER**

I MEAN, BACK IN HIGH SCHOOL, IF YOU HAD TOLD ME TEARING CLIENTS LIMB FROM LIMB WAS GOING TO BE IN MY JOB DESCRIPTION, I WOULD'VE SCOFFED--
HUH... SCOFFED, THERE'S A WORD MOST HIRED GOONS WOULDN'T USE IN CASUAL CONVERSATION.
BOY, IF YOU COULD'VE SEEN ME IN HIGH SCHOOL--
I WAS REALLY MAIN-LINING ACADEM-IA.
ARTIC SQUADRON
HONOR GUARD
HIGH CALIBER SOCIETY
COLLEGES WERE OFFERING ME SCHOLARSHIPS RIGHT AND LEFT.
EVEN THE PRESTIGIOUS GALACTIC U.
ARTIC SQUADRON
HONOR GUARD
SKIT!
HIGH CALIBER SOCIETY
I WAS GONNA BE A BIOCHEMIST.

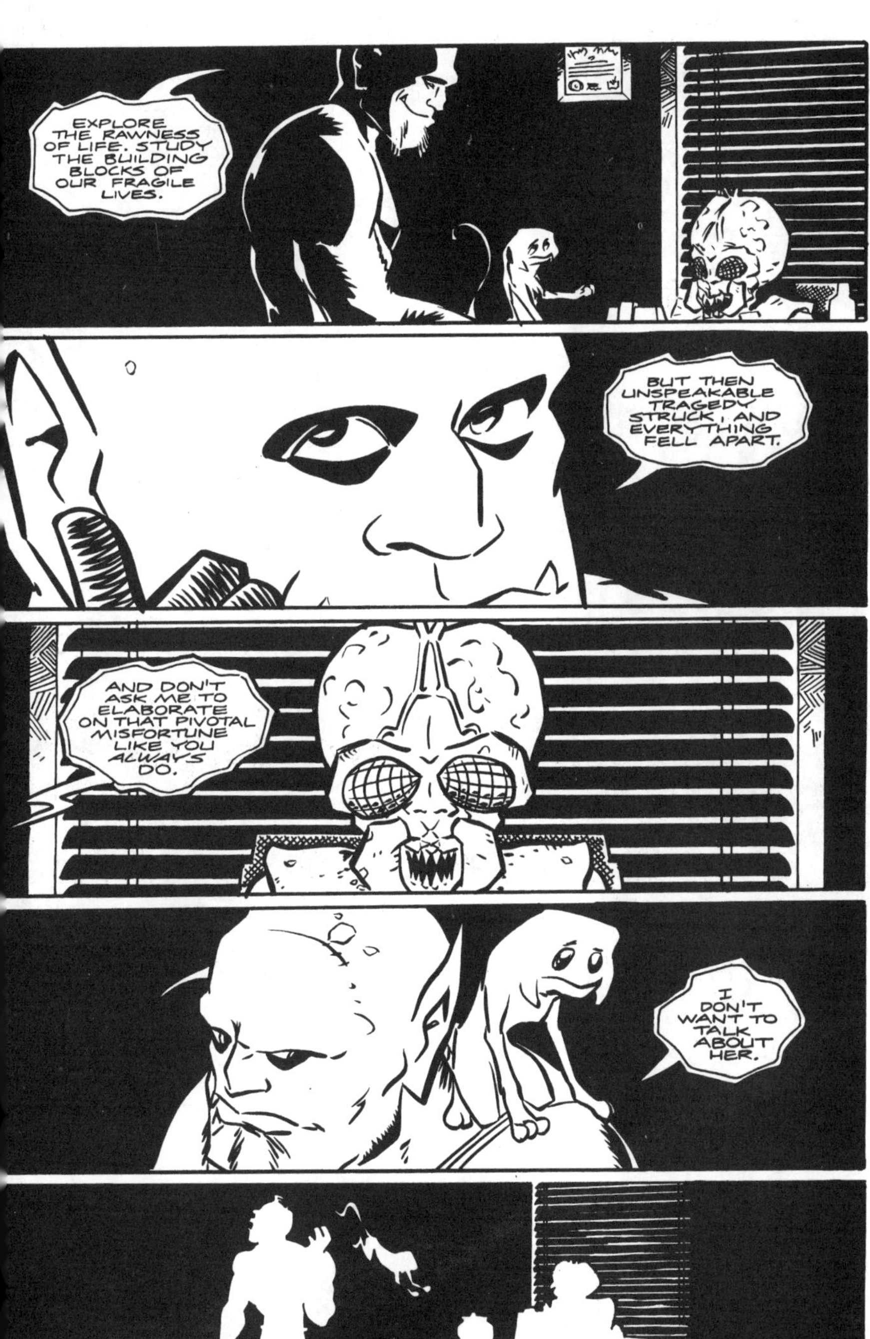
EXPLORE THE RAWNESS OF LIFE. STUDY THE BUILDING BLOCKS OF OUR FRAGILE LIVES.
BUT THEN UNSPEAKABLE TRAGEDY STRUCK, AND EVERYTHING FELL APART.
AND DON'T ASK ME TO ELABORATE ON THAT PIVOTAL MISFORTUNE LIKE YOU *ALWAYS* DO.
I DON'T WANT TO TALK ABOUT HER.

I FEEL SO INEFFECTUAL AND APATHETIC. EVEN MY MOST FUNDAMENTAL ASPIRATIONS ARE WANING.

MAYBE IT'S THE WHOLE LOSS OF INNOCENCE THING.
PERHAPS I'VE GIVEN ALL I HAVE TO GIVE.
I CAN'T EVEN WAX POETIC, FOR PETE'S SAKE.
CLIK!
CLIK
RINGGGGGG
WELL, I GUESS MY BREAKTHROUGH WILL HAVE TO WAIT 'TIL NEXT WEEK, EH, DOC?
HEY, YOU GOT SOME LOLLIPOPS!
HOPE YA DON'T MIND IF I HELP MYSELF. I LOVE THESE THINGS.

FAR OUT FANTASY, HEROIC HIJINXS AND WHIMSY THAT'S NOT FLIMSY ARE STAPLES OF TED TUCKER'S AND BRIAN CLOPPER'S COLLABORATIONS. FOR INFO ON THEIR FORTHCOMING PROJECT, GIDEON THUMP, E-MAIL THEM AT WINGNUTIBH@AOL.COM OR CAPHAP@AOL.COM. YOU CAN ALSO CONTACT THEM AT: BEHEMOTH BOOKS, BRIAN CLOPPER, 21 VALLEY PARK COURT, DAMASCUS, MD 20872 OR HAPPY INDUSTRIES, TED TUCKER, 921 FOREST HILL DR., CLERMONT, FL 34711.

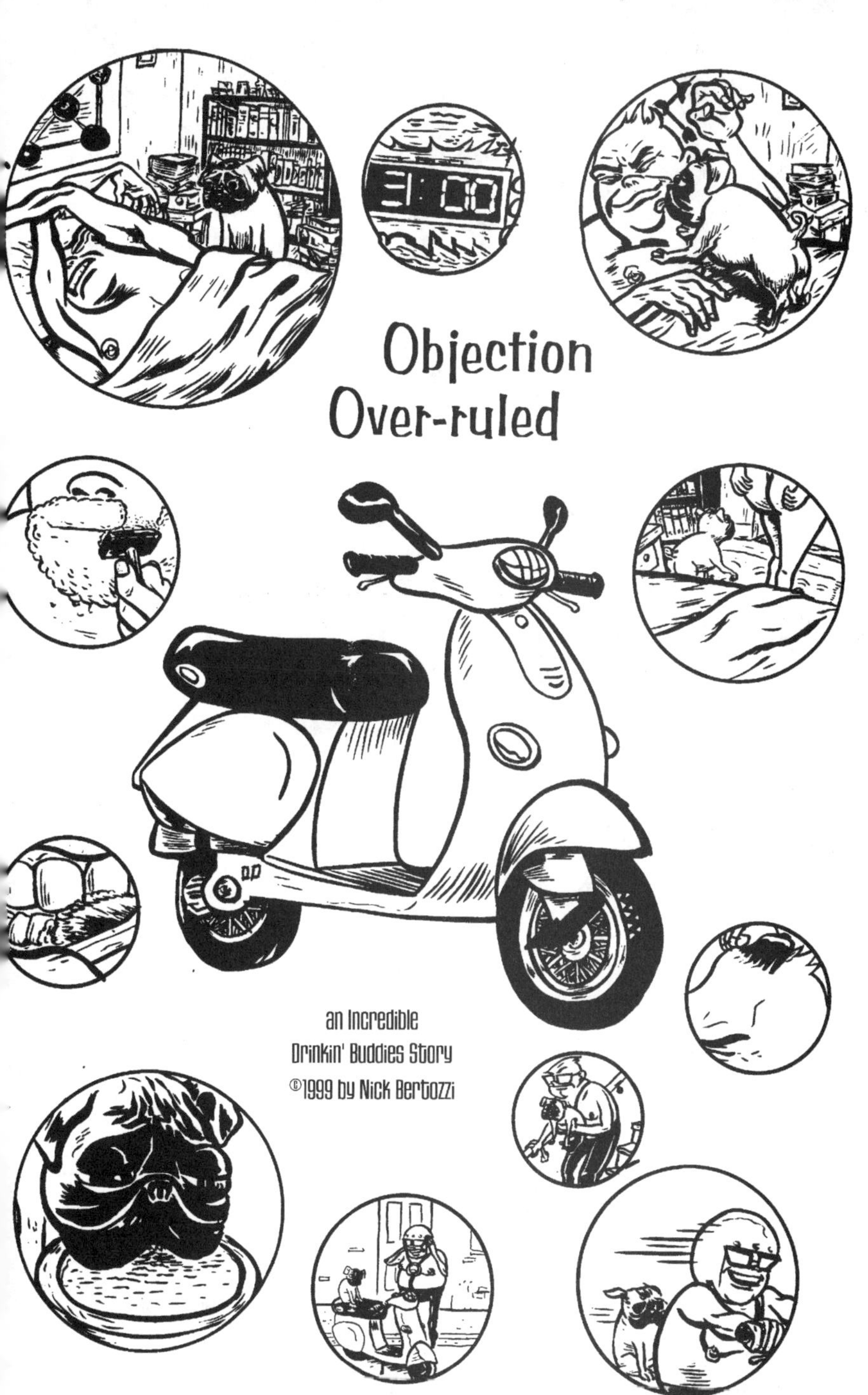

Objection Over-ruled

an Incredible
Drinkin' Buddies Story

I DID NOT ZINK FOR EVEN ONE MOMENT ZAT ZE FOOL VOULD ACTUALLY DO IT!
WELL, YOU DARED HIM, GUNTHER.
YEAH, MAN, THE FAT ONE NEEDS LITTLE COACHING AS IT IS.
WILL THE DEFENDANT PLEASE APPROACH THE BENCH.
DOCTOR CHAUNCY SAUCY.
YOU HAVE BEEN CHARGED BY THE PEOPLE OF THE COUNTY OF NEW YORK
WITH WILLFULLY DESTROYING PUBLIC PROPERTY WITH THE INTENT TO INCITE SUBVERSION.
GOD, I HOPE THAT MUNGO IS AS GOOD A LAWYER AS HE SAYS HE IS.
SAUCY BETTER NOT BE HIRING HIM JUST BECAUSE HE'S FAMILY.
IF MUNGO PRACTICES LAW LIKE THE WAY DOC DROVE HIS SCOOTER, I THINK WE'RE IN FOR A PRETTY WILD TRIAL.
YOU ARE ALSO CHARGED WITH RECKLESS DRIVING AND ENDANGERING THE PUBLIC.
ACH!
HE LOVED HIS SCOOTER! I JUST CANNOT BELIEVE IT!
BELIEVE IT! I WENT DOWN TO THE IMPOUND LOT AND IT IS FLAT AS A FRIGGIN' PANCAKE!
HE WAS DOIN' 70 WHEN HE HIT THE SCULPTURE, MAN!
LIKE...
BOOM!
HOW DO YOU PLEAD ON THESE COUNTS?

NOT GUILTY BY REASON OF AESTHETIC INSANITY, YOUR HONOR.
DOCTOR SAUCY, I CAUTION YOU: THIS IS A VERY SERIOUS MATTER AND SHOULD YOU BE FOUND GUILTY YOU WILL BE PUNISHED TO THE FULLEST EXTENT OF THE LAW.
HAVE YOU CONSULTED WITH YOUR ATTORNEY ABOUT YOUR PLEA?
YES, YOUR HONOR. THIS WAS MY BROTHER'S...
THIS PLEA WAS MY ATTORNEY'S IDEA!
MISTER SAUCY, I MUST ALSO GIVE YOU A WARNING.
YOU WILL NOT TURN THIS COURTROOM INTO A PLAYGROUND FOR YOUR OVER-INDULGENT IMAGINATION.
I URGE YOU TO TAKE ANOTHER TACK WITH THIS CASE. I THINK WE BOTH REMEMBER THE LAST TIME YOU HAD A CLIENT PLEAD INSANITY.
AHH... QUITE, QUITE.
I STILL HOLD BY THAT ONE, THOUGH. ANYONE DRIVING ELEVEN MILES OVER THE SPEED LIMIT MUST SURELY BE OUT OF THEIR MIND AND CANNOT BE HELD RESPONSIBLE FOR THEIR ACTIONS.
AND TO THINK HE HAD BEEN DRINKING! SHEAR MADNESS!
THAT IS UNFORTUNATELY YOUR OPINION, MISTER SAUCY. AND MAY I SAY THAT YOU WERE COMPLETELY ALONE IN THAT BELIEF.
I RECALL THAT THE JURY IN THAT CASE BROKE THE RECORD FOR THE SHORTEST DELIBERATION TIME IN THE HISTORY OF THE AMERICAN JUDICIAL SYSYTEM. 37 SECONDS, HM?
I'D RATHER THIS CASE DID NOT BECOME LEGEND, MUNGO. YOU SCREW UP AND I SWEAR I'LL HAVE YOU DISBARRED.
AYE, AYE, CAP'N!
STUPID JUDGE! THINKS HE KNOWS EVERYTHING!

parque
...AND IF SAUCY HADN'T LIKE, REFORMATTED THE GENETATOR RAY, EVERYONE IN BARCELONA WOULDA LOOKED LIKE PROFESSOR HATRED!
SO YOU CAN VOUCH FOR DOCTOR SAUCY'S CHARACTER BEING AN UPRIGHT AND NOBLE ONE, MISTER DEDUDE?
I CAN VOUCH WICKED STRONGLY.
THANK YOU, MISTER DEDUDE. NO MORE QUESTIONS.
AND WHAT EXACTLY WAS THE REACTION OF THE BARCELONESES?
SOME OF THEM ACTUALLY WANTED TO LOOK LIKE PROFESSOR HATRED, IF YOU CAN FRIGGIN' BELIEVE IT!
..YOU WERE THROWN OUT OF BARCELONA WITH THE WARNING: "DON'T COME BACKOR WE WILL HAVE YOU, STARTING WITH THE FAT ONE, TURNED INTO CHORIZO!"
SURE, IT SOUNDS AWFUL TAKEN LITERALLY, BUT THE BARCELONESES HAVE A REAL FONDNESS FOR THE DOCTOR.
"...WAS SEEN ATTEMPTING INTERCOURSE WITH A YARD SCULPTURE OF THE VIRGIN MARY."
ZE DOCTOR LIVES ON A HIGHER LEVEL, AND WE MUST RESPECT HIS MORE... ROBUST APETITES!
YES! IT IS ALL TRUE! BUT YOU SHOULD HAVE SEEN THE VIRGIN! SO IMMACULATE! SO CHASTE! SO IRRESISTABLE!

DAY 8
EXACTLY WHAT SORT OF DOCTOR ARE YOU, DOCTOR SAUCY?
FLUH-FLUH-FLUFF
WHAT'S THAT, DOCTOR? I'M AFRAID THE JURY CAN'T FOLLOW YOU.
I AM A DOCTOR OF COSMOLOGY!
AHH...
A DOCTOR OF THE SCIENCE OF COSMOLOGY. ENLIGHTEN ME, DOCTOR, FOR I AM A SIMPLE LAYPERSON...
PRAY TELL. WHAT, IN FACT, DOES THE SCIENCE OF COSMOLOGY STUDY?
IF YOU MUST KNOW, IT'S THE STUDY OF HAIR-FASHION AND MAKE-UP TECHNOLOGY.
THERE ARE SO MANY MOUSSES! YOU'D BE SURPRISED!
DOCTOR SAUCY! YOU WILL REFRAIN FROM DIRECTING YOUR ANSWERS TO THE JURY!
NOW, "DOCTOR". WHERE DID YOU TAKE YOUR DEGREE?
BARBIZON. I WAS FIRST IN MY CLASS!
YOU SHOULD'VE SEEN ME! I WAS A DEMON WITH A SET OF CLIPPERS! I COULD TAKE THE MOST HIDEOUS MEDUSA AND TRANSFORM HER INTO THE MOST RESPLENDENT APHRODITE!
TELL US, DOCTOR. YOU WERE FIRST IN YOUR CLASS AND YET BARBIZON HAS NO RECORD OF YOU FINISHING YOUR DEGREE...
OH, DON'T YOU BELIEVE IT!
THE OTHER STUDENTS WERE JEALOUS OF ME! SOMEONE SLIPPED "HAIR-OFF" INTO MY GEL BOTTLE AS I WAS STYLING THE DEAN'S WIFE!
DOC-TOR SAUCY! YOU MUST ADDRESS THE PROSECUTING ATTORNEY!
I WAS FRAMED! FRAMED!
I WAS EXPELLED THAT NIGHT...

DAY 10
I AM AN ARTIST, AND THAT SHOULD BE MY PARDON.
I NECESSARILY WORK WITHIN THE WORLD OF DREAMS, CHANNELS OF THOUGHT.
MY PAINTINGS ARE BRUSHED INTO THE FOLDS OF YOUR MIND
MY SCULPTIRES ARE MOLDED SO THAT THEY AFFIX THEMSELVES TO YOUR MEDULLA OBLONGOTA.
THIS MOVEMENT IS NOT INTERESTED IN PRICE, NOR GALLERY SHOWS, NOR MUSEUMS.
ALONG WITH THE INCREDIBLE DRINKIN' BUDDIES I CREATE CEREBRAL PICTURES, WE CRAFT MESSAGES FROM THE ETHER.
THIS IS THE SPIRIT IN WHICH I DESTROYED PUBLIC SCULPTURE #109!
MAN, HE'S GOOD!
I HAD TO DESTROY IN ORDER TO BUILD!
I DID THIS FOR YOU!
WE DON'T HAVE TO LIVE WITH THESE UGLY AND BUREAUCRATIC SCULPTURES ANYMORE!
THIS DESTRUCTION WAS A WORK OF ART THAT SAID: "HEY! BUDDY! YOU TOO HAVE THE RIGHT AND THE POWER TO TAKE ON THE WORLD ALL BY YOURSELF!"
SCREAM "ANARCHIST" TO THE ROOFTOPS IF YOU WANT!
BUT KNOW THIS: WHAT I DID IS ONLY THE FIRST STEP IN A NEW DEMOCRACY!
THE FIRST STEP IN YOUR NEW LUXURY CAR CALLED "FREEDOM"!
IT'S ROLLING OFF THE ASSEMBLY LINE OF SELF-ENLIGHTENMENT RIGHT NOW! JUST WAITING FOR YOU TO BUY IT WITH THE FRESH GREEN DOLLARS OF SELF-ESTEEM!
DOC-TOR SAUCY! CONTAIN YOURSELF!
CONTAIN YOUR OWN MIND, YOU BUTT-SUCKING ROBOT!
ORDER! ORDER! BAILIFF!
YOU DON'T HAVE TO DO THIS, BOYS!
THIS IS A CHARADE!
IT IS YOUR IRREALITY!
HOLD THE LITTLE FAGGOT STILL, GODDAMNIT!
NNG!
AWAKEN, CHILDREN OF TELEVISION AND CONVENIENCE!
HASTEN UNTO ME AND I SHALL LEAD THEE INTO PARADISE!
GKK!

ALL RISE.
PLEASE BE SEATED.
LADIES AND GENTLEMEN OF THE JURY
WE HAVE HEARD ALL THE TESTIMONY IN THIS CASE AND WE HAVE EVEN HEARD FROM THE DEFENDANT HIMSELF
IT IS NOW TIME FOR THE CLOSING STATEMENTS
PLEASE GIVE US THOSE STATEMENTS, MISS TWOSHOES.
THANK YOU, YOUR HONOR.
MY FRIENDS.
YOU ARE SITTING IN THAT BOX BECAUSE IT IS YOUR DUTY TO PASS JUDGEMENT ON ONE OF YOUR PEERS.
HOWEVER, I MUST ASK YOU:
DOES THIS MAN THINK OF HIMSELF AS YOUR PEER?
IS HE REALLY CONCERNED WITH YOUR CHILDREN'S FUTURE, OR IS HE JUST ANOTHER HAIRDRESSING VANDAL WITH A LOT OF BIG IDEAS?
WELL, YOU HEARD HIM SPEAK FOR YOURSELVES AND HONESTLY
HEH-HEH
I CAN'T ADD A THING!
I'M GOING TO STOP WASTING YOUR TIME, MY FRIENDS
I BELIEVE THAT YOU CAN MAKE UP YOUR OWN MINDS ABOUT THIS BAD, BAD MAN!
RIGHT ON!
YOU'RE DAMN RIGHT WE CAN THINK FOR OURSELVES!
HANG THE SICK LITTLE MONKEY!
STRING HIM UP RIGHT NOW!

NO PUNK. I DON'T WANT TO PLAY RIGHT NOW.
MAYBE WE COULD TIE SOME ROPE TO HIS CELL BARS AND BUST HIM FREE WITH A TRACTOR-TRAILER.
MY COUSIN REG HAS THIS HUGE TRUCK!
NAHHH.
I SUPPOSE I COULD JUST USE MY FEMININE WILES AND JUST *WALTZ IN THERE* AND BRIBE THE GUARD WITH KISSES!
NEIN.
NO...
NOPE.
SLUR

DON'T WORRY, CHAUNCY! I THINK THEY'RE STARTING TO COME AROUND!
COME AROUND!?!
THEY'RE READY TO HANG ME!
OH, WHY DID I LET MOM TALK ME INTO THIS?
"HE'S A GOOD LAWYER!"
"HE'S WON SEVERAL OF THE CASES HE'S TRIED!"
"HE'S ALMOST NEVER LATE WITH HIS ALIMONY PAYMENTS!"
"HE'S BEEN OUT OF REHAB FOR THREE MONTHS!"
OH, KHEE-RIST!
C'MON, SAUCY!
THIS IS JUST MY COME-FROM-BEHIND STRATEGY!
I PROMISE I'LL GET YOU OFF!
...OR GET YOUR SENTENCE REDUCED...
...OR GET YOU THOSE CHOCOLATES THAT YOU LIKE...
SHRIEK!
HEY!
I COULD EVEN TRY FOR ONE OF THOSE MISSED TRIALS!
YEAH!
YOU'LL SEE!
I'M GOING TO JAIL FOREVER!
WAAHHH!
C'MON, CHAUNCY! DON'T BE SO UPSET!
REMEMBER WHEN WE WERE KIDS AND I WAS BABYSITTING YOU? AND ME AN TONY GONZALVES WERE SO HIGH FROM HUFFING GAS THAT I DIDN'T EVEN NOTICE WHEN YOU PUT YOUR HEAD THROUGH THAT PLATE-GLASS WINDOW IN THE LIVING ROOM?
WELL, WHO TAKE CARE OF YOU THEN, HUNH?
I SOBERED UP AND WRAPPED GAUZE AROUND YOUR HEAD AND SANG YOU THAT SONG THAT YOU LOVED
WHAT WAS THAT SONG?
"FOR YOUR EYES ONLY"

OH YEAH!
LET'S SEE...
HOW'S THAT GO AGAIN?
"FOR YOUR EYES ONLY/ CAN SEE ME THROUGH THE NIGHT!"
BEE-BOO BEE-BOO
"FOR YOUR EYES ONLY/ I NEVER NEED TO HIDE"
BEE-BOO BEE-BOO
GET AWAY FROM ME!
"YOU CAN SEE SO MUCH IN ME THAT'S NEW..."
"...I NEVER FELT UNTIL I LOOKED AT YOU."
"FOR YOUR EYES ON-LEE!"
"ON-LEE FOR YOU!"
"YOU'LL SEE WHAT NO ONE ELSE CAN SEE..."
"NOW I'M BREAKING FREE!"
"FOR YOUR EYES ON-LEEEE..."

LADIES AND GENTLEMEN OF THE JURY, I ASK YOUR FORGIVENESS FOR WHAT I AM ABOUT TO SAY.
I WANTED TO AVOID THIS ROUTE. YOU WON'T LIKE IT, AND YOU MAY EVEN FIND IT EMBARASSING, BUT IT'S THE ONLY WAY THAT WE CAN SAVE THIS POOR MAN, DOCTOR CHAUNCY SAUCY.
I LET CHAUNCY TELL YOU THAT HE DESTROYED PUBLIC BEAUTIFICATION PROJECT #309-HP66 BECAUSE IT OFFENDED HIS AESTHETIC SENSE..
WELL, THAT WAS COMPLETE B.S.!
CHAUNCY WOULDN'T KNOW A PICASSO IF IT BIT HIM ON THE ASS!
NO.
THE REAL REASON IS THAT:
HE WANTED TO COPULATE WITH THE SCULPTURE.
DEAR LORD, NO!
SHOCKING! SIMPLY SHOCKING!
NO, GOOD PEOPLE OF THE JURY, YOU DON'T SEE A DANGEROUS LUNATIC IN FRONT OF YOU.
YOU HAVE INSTEAD, A HARMLESS LITTLE MAN WHO WAS PUSHED TO THE BRINK OF INSANITY BY HIS INSATIABLE LUST!
HE WAS TORMENTED BY A... DARE I SAY IT?
A MONSTROUS VAGINA!
OBSCENE, HORRIBLE, VILE SCULPTURE!
I MEAN, LOOK AT IT, PEOPLE!
DEAR GOD, HE'S RIGHT!
FILTH! PURE FILTH!
THE SCULPTOR SHOULD BE SHOT!
WHAT ABOUT THE CHILDREN?!
HE'S NOT A SCULPTOR-HE'S A PORNOGRAPHER!

AND THERE IT WAS TAUNTING HIM EVERY DAY!
QUESTIONING HIS MANHOOD!
DEBILITATING HIM!
FOR HEAVEN'S SAKE, PEOPLE! EVEN MY GRANDFATHER USED TO TELL ME HE'D GET RANDY EVERY TIME HE WALKED BY IT!
AND RATHER THAN LOSE CONTROL AND GIVE IN TO HIS BASEST DESIRES, MY CLIENT CHOSE TO DESTROY THIS LOATHESOME MONUMENT!
MY GOD, PEOPLE! HAVE YOU NEVER BEEN HORNY?
FOR YOU TO CON-VICT CHAUNCY SAUCY...
WELL... YOU WOULD BE PUTTING YOURSELVE IN LEAGUE WITH THE PORNOGRAPHER PERVERTS AND THE EVIL POLITICIANS WHO BUILT THAT HORRID SCULPTURE!
LADIES AND GENTLEMEN OF THE JURY, IT IS YOUR CHOICE
YEAH! TESTIFY, BROTHER!
I WAS HORNY ONCE TOO!
HE DID IT FOR THE CHILDREN!
LET'S SMASH SOMETHING!

Kuh-sMASsh!

ONCH-OONCH-OONCH-OONCH-OONCH-OON

THE END

the incredible mini-biddies

Blast from the Past

MY HOW TIME FLIES, NO? SEEMS LIKE ONLY AN ISSUE AGO WE WERE YOUNG, CAREFREE BUCKS.
YEAH, AND I DIDN'T HAVE A NEED FOR CAREFREE MAXI-PADS, EITHER. AND NOW THAT I'VE GONE THROUGH THE "CHANGE OF LIFE," I DON'T NEED 'EM AGAIN.
THE MORE THINGS CHANGE, THE MORE THEY STAY THE SAME. HEY DON,T YOU MEAN STAYFREE?
THE OLD GRAY MARE AIN'T, SHE WHAT SHE USED TO BE, KNOW WHAT I'M SAYIN'?

SPEAKING OF OLD GRAY MARES AND MAXI-PADS, YOU STILL USING THOSE DARN THINGS, SAUCY?

YEP. DON'T SEE ANY REASON TO SPEND ALL THAT MONEY ON THEM "ADULT" DIAPERS, WHEN A WELL PLACED MAXI-PAD CAN ABSORB MY LITTLE LEAKS WITH NO SEEPAGE.
MAYBE I SHOULD DO THAT, TOO. IT'D MAKE ME FEEL YOUNG AGAIN, EVEN IF THE BODY FLUID IS DRIBBLING FROM THE WRONG ORIFICE.
I PREFER TAMPONS UP MY POPO, BUT THAT'S JUST ME.

WAITAMINUTE! NOOOO! IT CAN'T BE...
SPEAKING OF "THE MORE THINGS CHANGE" TYPE SCENARIOS...
I CAN'T BELIEVE IT. IT'S...
ENOUGH WITH THE ELLIPSES, IT'S (OH WHAT THE HECK)
...
BRONCO!
NOW REMEMBER WHAT I SAID, MR. BUCEPHALUS NO EXCITEMENT FOR YOU, LEST YOUR POOR, WEE, FRAIL TICKER WILL GIVE YOU A NASTY OLD HEART-ATTACKY.
I UNDERSTAND, NURSIE. I'LL JUST SIT ON THIS BENCH AND REST.
HEWWO, WITTLE BIRDIE.
HOW ARE YOU TODAY?
COOCHIE-COOCHIE-COO.
OH! TEE-HEE!
SPLORT!
THE CALL OF NATURE WAITS FOR NEITHER MAN, NOR BEAST, EH WEE BIRDIE?

HEE-HEE. YESIREE, BOB, BOY-O...HEH, HEH.
CALL OF NATURE. THAT'S A GOOD ONE.
HELLO, BRONCO!
GAAAGH!
PLLLUURRRRBBSCHT!
WHAT? WHO?
OH FOR CRIMINY SAKES. NOEXCITEMENT.
YOU!
FLIBBERTY-GEE, I THOUGHT I'D NEVER SEE YOU HOOLIGA-NE'ER-DO WELLS AG'IN! CONSARN IT! YOU GAVE ME SUCH A START I PLUM FILLED UP M' DRAWERS WITH OFFAL.
GEE, BRONCO, WE'D HAVE THOUGHT YOU'D BE HAPPY TO HEAR FROM OLD FRIENDS.
YEAH, BRONCSKI-BEAT.
THAT EXPLAINS THE OFFAL SMELL.
WHAT AN OFFAL JOKE.
OFFALLY SORRY, OLD CHAP. AND I DO MEAN OLD.

LOOKIT, THIS ISN'T KINDY-GARTEN NO MORE.
I'VE LEARNED A THING OR TWO ABOUT A THING OR TWO, AND I'LL TELL YOU WHAT: I'VE BEEN TOLD NOT TO GET EXCITED AND YOU'RE EXCITING ME!
I,M EXCITING YOU?
IS THAT TRUE? WHAT YOU SAID?
NOW YOU KNOW THAT'S NOT WHAT I MEANT. I MEANT NOTHING SLAUCY... I MEAN SAGACIOUS... GROAN ... I MEAN SAUCY.
SAUCY'S WHAT I'M LOOKING FOR.
HOO-HOO!
THINGS,VE CHANGED, EH, BRONCO?
I NEVER KNEW YOU SKEWED TO THE HELLENIC LOVE CURVE, BRONKY-SWUNG WITH THE FRIENDS OF LIZA AS IT WERE.
COME VIZ ME, DAHLINK, AND I SHOW YOU ZE FORBIDDEN FRUITS...
AND HE DOES MEAN FRUITS.
THIS IS KEY WEST, AFTER ALL.
THE WORD "SAUCY!" I MEANT THE WORD, NOT YOU, YOU PREENING PRE-VERT!
NOW YOU'VE HURT MY FEELINGS, YOU HUGE-HEADED HETEROCLITE!

FOR SEVENTY YEARS I'VE BEEN MERCIFULLY FREE OF YOUR MISERABLE COMPANY, AND NOW IN MY TWILIGHT YEARS I NOW FIND MYSELF THE VICTIM OF YOUR SHENANIGANS AGAIN!
WELL, ENOUGH I SAY! THUS FAR AND NO FURTHER!
YOU'LL NOT MAKE BRONCO BUCEPHALUS YOUR GOAT AGAIN!
LAND O' GOSHEN, YOU CREEPY COOTS'LL BE THE DEATH OF ME...
MY HEART!
MY PILLS!
GUUUUHHHH!
HEY DIDN'T THAT NURSE TELL HIM NOT TO GET EXCITED?
YEAH, BRONCO NEVER WAS MUCH GOOD AT FOLLOWING SUGGESTIONS.
HE SHOULD'VE "CHUST VOLLOWED ORDERZ, JA?"
DID HE SAY SOMETHING ABOUT PILLS?
end!

THERE COMES A TIME IN THE LIFE OF EVERY BUG WHEN THE WORLD SHATTERS INTO PIECES AND NOTHING MAKES SENSE ANYMORE.

THERE COULD BE A HUNDRE MILLION REASONS WHY. MAYBE YOUR WIFE WILL LEAVE YOU. OR MAYBE YOU'LL LEAVE HER.

NO BUG IS CLEVER ENOUG TO FIT THE PIECES BACK TOGETHER THE WAY THEY WE

THIS IS YOUR CHANCE TO PUT THE PIECES BACK TOGETHER IN A NEW ORDER, TO REBUILD THE WORLD HOWEVER YOU SEE FIT

DON'T KILL YOURSELF

ONCE ALL THE CRYING AND SHAKING AND HIDING UNDER THE BED IS OVER YOU WILL MUSTER UP A LITTLE COURAGE TO LOOK AROUND

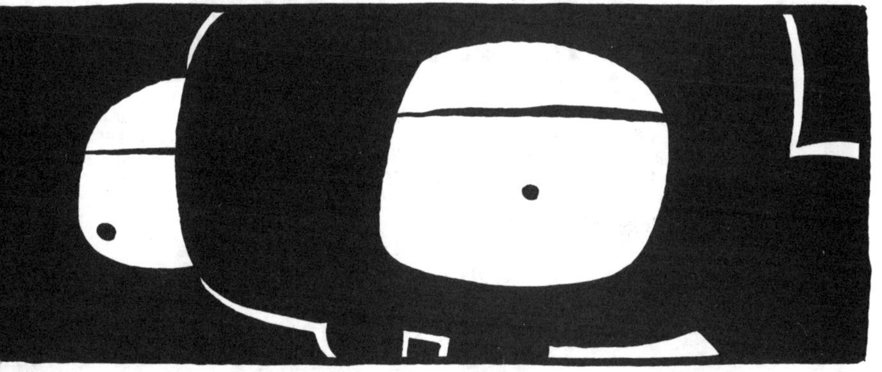

YEAH, THE WORLD MAY BE IN RUINS AROUND YOU, BUT YOU CAN'T HELP BUT NOTICE YOU HAVE SURVIVED

ALIVE! THAT'S A GOOD PLACE TO START!

JAMES KOCHALKA

stanley the SUBURBAN GANGSTA

YO, YO, YO, MY MAN, whazzup which you, YO??? MY NAME's STANLEY, AND i'm one HARDASS Mutha Fuckin' G!!!

SURPRISED YA NEVER HEARD OF ME, KID!! YAKNOW, I GOTTA REP N' SHIT, I'M FROM the STREETS, YO...

... Yeah, the HARDASS streets of SCOTTSDALE!!! Yo, check this SHIT out, KID! Just got BACK FROM the Fuckin' MAll with MY MOMS AND YO, Peep this...

... she Fuckin' BOUGHT ME the NEWEST, illist, TOMMY HIL-FIGER shit, some NEW $450.00 NIKES, and yo.... CHECK it.. A 24 carot WU WEAR Fuckin' NECKLACE, yo!!!

YOU KNOW how MANY mutha FuckAS would kill their OWN MAMA FOR one of these Kid?? SHIT, YEA... YOU KNOW where i'M comin' From, huh? Yea, word...

YO MAN, did I MENTION that I'M Also AN M.C., kid? Yea, I got MAD Rhymes, yo. Matter of Fact, I'm goin' down to NITA's ON THURSDAY night, and I'M GONNA Fuckin' challenge that Fuckin' kid PUMA to A battle and blah blah blah

YEA, just give ME A FATASS chRONIC BLUNT AND I'll get up on stage AND RIP SHIT, YA KNOW? Word, just got my FIRST GUN the other day Kid!! Hell yea, NOW Nobody's GONNA STEP TO ME...

So yo Kid, what the Fuck You DOIN' READin' A BOOK, N' shit?? YO, I go straight to the SOURCE FOR MY INFO AND KNOWLEDGE... PUFF DADDY AND TUPAC, kid, KNOW what I'M SAYIN, Yo??

Yo, where da Fuck you goin' MAN?? I'M still talkin' HERE!!! SHIT... HEY YO, come back HERE, KID!! I GOTTA FAT SACK OF WEED IN MY pocket, YO! c'MON we'll get MAD BLUNTED N' SHIT!! Yea, think I'M GONNA start DEALIN' n shit, too hell yea i blah blah blah bla

A 40Z. COMICS PRODUCTION

true tales of Amerikkkan history

HOW the WEST WAS Actvally WON...
DADDY, WHO ARE those STRANGE MEN?
I... I DON'T KNOW, MY CHILD.

HEY THERE, HOW'S IT GOING?
WE'RE WHITE CHRISTIAN males, AND we're here to claim this land for ourselves...

EXCUSE ME?? uh... well, we were here First AND...
Yeah, So?

ACCORDING to this piece OF PAPER, issued by the government we just set up, we OWN THIS LAND...
FAKE CONTRACT BY U.S. GOV.

BUT...
I SUGGEST you comply MY FRIEND, or we'll be FORCED TO USE OUR BOOMSTICKS.

BOOM STICKS??
?

YEAH, CHECK THIS OUT...
BLAM!
BLAM!

AAARRGHHH

DADDY!! NO!!!

DON'T BE SAD, Little GIRL. WE'RE NOT HERE TO ENSLAVE YOUR PEOPLE, WE'RE HERE TO SAVE THEM...

YEAH, THAT'S RIGHT. WE'RE GOING TO INTRODUCE YOUR PEOPLE TO THE JOYS OF DEMOCRACY + COMMERCE! WE'LL INTRODUCE YOU TO OUR LIQUOR, DRUGS, AND FIREARMS! WE'LL TEACH YOU HOW TO LIE, CHEAT, STEAL, + STAB YOUR OWN BROTHER IN THE BACK. WE'LL TEACH YOU HOW TO RAPE + PILAGE THE LAND, TAKING WHATEVER YOU WANT...

BASICALLY, WE'RE PRETTY MUCH GONNA FUCK YOUR PEOPLE OVER FOR THE NEXT 5 TO 600 YEARS..

JOHN... DON'T SAY THAT!! HEH, HEH... WHAT HE MEANT TO SAY IS THAT IT'S ALL IN THE NAME OF PROGRESS, HONEY... OH YEAH... AND JESUS... WE CAN'T FORGET ABOUT JESUS...

NEXT TIME: witness HOW the BRAVE CHRISTIAN SOLDIERS FEARLESSLY ENSLAVE OVER 2 MILLION AFRICANS! ALL IN the NAME OF AMERIKKKA! YES!!

Stupid Comics
©98 JIM MAHFOOD

NO TIME...

JIM, hey this is ROBERT FROM JAVA. uh, listen, heh, heh, I sorta Forgot to give you A DEADLINE FOR the NEW COMIC AND uh... I SORTA NEED it by tomorrow.... you think you can get it DONE BY then...?
uh....

JIM, what's up, this is KEVIN SMITH. Listen MAN, I KNOW that script I PROMISED you FOR the new CLERKS book is like FOUR WEEKS LATE, but I swear.... you should have it by the end OF the WEEK! HopeFully, you'll have time to DRAW the Fuckin' Book. say, when you comin' out to JERSEY to visit?
WELL, I think that...

YO JIM, what up MY ARAB NIGGA! Yo, this is EMILE!! Listen Kid, I got YA SOME MORE FLYER WORK iF YA WANNIT, dig? Listen, let's go get LIQUORED UP AND check out SOME HOOKERS, YO!!!
MAN, i'd LOVE TO, BUT RIGHT NOW I'M SORTA FUCKED ON DEADLINES...

JIMMY, this is YOUR MOTHER, sweety. WHY haven't you called ME IN the last couple of WEEKS? I KNOW you're extremely busy honey, but this is ridiculous.... I still don't KNOW WHY YOU moved all the way out to ARIZONA.... HAVE YOU FOUND A girlFRIEND OR Met ANYONE Special yet? You Really need to blah blah blah blah..
OH, GOD..

YO, YO, YO!! JIM, MY MAN, what da FUCK is up which YOU, SON?? Yo, this is DJ POSER, kid!! YEAH, I don't KNOW iF YA Remember, but I met YA AT BOSTON'S LIKE 2 MONTHS AGO, SON. ANY WAY, I WAS just wonderin' iF you'd HAVE TIME to do A COVER FOR MY NEW MIX TAPE!! YO, AND blah blah
HOW the FUCK did you GET MY NUMBER?!!

HEY JIM, what's up dude? This is RUSSELL FROM SWELL. Just wonderin' iF you'll still have time to do that ALBUM COVER FOR ME. ALSO, SNAIL AND LISA WANNA KNOW why you NEVER Return THEIR calls. They think you're Actin' like A self-centered PRICK.... Just thought I'D LET YA KNOW, MAN..
GOOD GRIEF.

JIM, hey kid, whazzup, this is CHUCK AMOK!! WHAT THE FUCK IS WRONG WITH YOU MAN??!! YOU NEVER RETURN MY CALLS AND I HAVEN'T SEEN YOU IN WEEKS... I still NEED TO CHECK out YOUR NEW PLACE. HEY, LET'S GET TOGETHER and smoke A BOWL And WATCH SOME CARTOONS AND THEN WE CAN
DAMN, i'd LIKE TO BUT....

JIM, this is the SCHRECK. where the HELL are those NEW ZOMBIE KID PAGES, MAN??!! I Need UM by tomorrow, kid! Also, COMICS SCENE MAGAZINE wants to do AN interview with you but you NEED to call them by 3:30 PM today OR they don't WANNA DO IT SO, YA KNOW...
GRRRR...
JIM, how's it GOING, MAN? THIS IS MARTY. LISTEN, I'VE GOT FOX MTV AND comedy CENTRAL All looking at your stuff for possible animation deals! I'M tellin' you KID, this is it!!!!! WERE GONNA MAKE YOU FAMOUS, KID!! This is just the BEGINNING OF Blah Blah Blah Blah Blah Blah
SOMEBODY SHOOT ME NOW...

SCOTTSDALE BABY VS. FRATBOY BABY

WAAAAHH!!! 'M A LITTLE ELF-CENTERED BRAT FROM COTTSDALE!! VERYBODY PAY TTENTION TO ME!!!
WAAAAHH!!! I'M A LITTLE UNORIGINAL BRAINLESS FRAT BOY!! EVERYONE LISTEN TO ME!!!
BUD LIGHT
I'VE NEVER WORKED A DAY IN MY LIFE AND MY PARENTS PAY FOR EVERYTHING!! I'VE REALLY GOT IT ROUGH!!!
I'M AN INSECURE DORK WHOSE MAIN CONCERN IS GAINING THE ACCEPTANCE OF MY FRATBOY BROTHERS, WHO ARE ALSO INSECURE DORKS!!!
GREEK SHIT
ΩΠ
MY '97 PATHFINDER IS A YEAR OLD!! I NEED A NEW ONE!!! WAAAAHH!!
I DIDN'T GET TO WATCH ALL SIX FOOTBALL GAMES THAT WERE ON TV YESTERDAY BECAUSE I HAD TO FIND SOMEONE TO WRITE MY HISTORY PAPER!!!! WAAAAH!!
ASU

HERE'S MINORITIES SLOWLY AKING OVER MY NEIGHBORHOOD!! NIGGERS AND DIRTY MEXICANS, I TELL YA!! WAAAHH!! I HATE ANYONE THAT ISN'T A POSTER BOY FOR THE ARYAN RACE!!!
ME TOO!!
WHITE POWER
MY MOM WON'T BUY ME A JET SKI!! I THINK I'LL OVERDOSE ON SPEED AND END UP IN THE HOSPITAL JUST TO TEACH THAT DUMB BITCH A LESSON!!
I HAVEN'T GOTTEN LAID IN DAYS!! I'VE GOTTA FIND SOME IMPRESSIONABLE FRESHMAN GIRL THAT I CAN GET DRUNK AND TAKE ADVANTAGE OF!!!!
I ♥ TITS
WAAAAHH!!! OUR STUPID FUCKING MAID LOST ONE OF MY FAVORITE POLOS!! I'LL KILL THAT SLUT, I SWEAR!!
MY ENGLISH TEACHER'S MAKING US READ POETRY!! I HATE THAT ART FAG-TYPE SHIT!! AND SPEAKING OF FAGS, I HATE THEM TOO!!
YEAH!!
NIKE WHORE

SPEND ALL MY IME WATCHING ABLE AND COLLECTING ANYTHING WITH "TOMMY HILFIGER" ON IT!! WAAAAHH!! MY LIFE IS SO HARD!!
I SPEND ALL MY TIME LIFTING WEIGHTS TO COMPENSATE FOR THE FACT THAT I HAVE A SMALL DICK!! OH YEAH- AND DRINKING SHITTY BEER... LIKE BUD LIGHT AND COORS AND SO ON AND SO FORTH...
FOOTBALL ROCKS
MY GIRLFRIEND'S AS THOUGHTLESS AND UNORIGINAL AS I AM!! SHE'S A SNOBBY, STUCK-UP BITCH, BUT I GUESS I'LL KEEP DATING HER CAUSE SHE'S THE HOTTEST GIRL IN TOWN!! YEAH!!!
PUFF DADDY'S THE GREATEST RAPPER EVER!! I DON'T KNOW ANYTHING ABOUT REAL HIP HOP, BUT I KNOW PUFFY'S THE SHIT BECAUSE THE RADIO TOLD ME SO!!!
PUFF DADDY
WAAAAHH!!! ALL THIS CRYING CAN'T BE GOOD FOR MY COMPLEXION!! I'D BETTER GO TO THE SALON AND PAY FIFTY DOLLARS FOR A HAIR CUT, THEN I'LL GO TO THE MALL AND BLAH BLAH BLAH
WAAAHH!!!! I'D BETTER GET BACK TO THE FRAT-HOUSE SO MY OLDER FRAT BROTHERS CAN TREAT ME LIKE SHIT!! I KNOW IT'S UNFAIR, BUT I'LL DO ANYTHING FOR THEIR ACCEPTANCE!!!
BRAIN WASHED

CUPID IS A FUCKED UP BASTARD

©99 JIM MAHFOOD

ALLY LOVES TO MASTURBATE

hazzup, WALLY? ow'd YA do n that Math est today?
Not so good, I'M AFRAID. I stayed up All Night MASTURBATING to the NEW ISSUE OF PLAYBOY...

HUH??
YA see, the new issue Features A girl FROM ARIZONA! that's Right, she's FROM MESA! oh, how I wish that she were MY GIRLFRIEND...

I SEE...
WELL, I'D Better get goin HOME NOW. I JUST picked up the NEW ISSUE OF "JAVA", AND I CAN'T WAIT to JERK OFF while I look at the HOT CHICKS in the "MARZ" Ads...

ARENCE the big Fat Fuckin computer nerd

LARONCE, DID YOU TAKE UT the TRASH LIKE I ASKED YOU?!! it's started to rot...
NOT YET, MOM...

DID YOU DO YOUR HOMEWORK?? DID YOU FEED the DOG???
I'M SURFin' the net, MOM...

DIDN'T I tell you to GET AWAY FROM the COMPUTER FOR AT LEAST 20 MINUTES A DAY?? WHY don't you go OUT AND TRY TO MAKE SOME REAL FRIENDS...
got everything I NEED RIGHT HERE, MOM...

AN I STICK THIS SPATULA UP YOUR ASS?

OKAY THEN.
YOUR LOSS.

HUH???

BOX OFFICE POISON 2000

©1999 Alex Robinson

When we last left our hero, Sherman was surrounded by an angry hoard o K'Ustom'rs, aliens so stupid they don' know Uranus-from their elbows!

DO YOU WORK HERE? SIR?
DO YOU WORK HERE?
BLAST IT, ED! WHERE ARE YOU?
CAN YOU HELP ME?

HEY! SORRY I'M LATE!
I GOT STUCK IN TH FREAK METEOR STO NEAR ALDERAAN.
YOU READY?
LET'S GO!!

:SIGH: I HAVE TO GET A NEW WORK DETAIL.
EVERYDAY I TELL MYSELF THEY CAN'T GET ANY DUMBER, BUT THEN THEY SURPRISE YOU.
TODAY, ONE OF THEM ASKED IF WE SOLD DATA TAPES ON VIRTU-O VACATIONS TO THE KUBRICK NEBULA! CAN YOU BELIEVE THAT?
YOU THINK THAT'S BAD?

"I HAD TO SPEND ALL DAY FIXING MR. FLAVOR'S ROBO BODY WHILE HE YELLED AT ME. I SHOULD'VE PUT SO SUGAR IN HIS ISOLINEAR CONVERTER, THE OLD COOT.

HEY! WATCH IT WITH THAT HYDRO-SPANNER!

SPEAKING OF WHICH WHEN WAS THE LAST TIME YOU WENT OUT IN YOUR REAL BODY?
I KNOW, I KNOW...

BUT MY REAL BODY IS LIKE 800 POUNDS NOW. I'M TOO EMBARRASSED TO BE SEEN.
WHAT TIME AR WE MEETING DOROTHY?

"AT 6:30 AT CHALMUN'S CANTINA ON TALOS IV..."
OH, SWEETIE! THANK THE MAKER YOU MADE IT!
WHY? WHAT'S UP?
I-- I THINK SOMEONE'S HIRED A BOUNTY HUNTER TO KILL ME!!
WHAT?!

IT'S TRUE! I WAS SHOPPING ON THE PROMENADE AT ORD MANTELL WHEN THIS GUY POPS UP AND STARTS SHOOTING PHOTON BEAMS AT ME!"

"LUCKILY, I HAD A TELETRANSPORT CHARGE ON ME SO I MOLECULIZED OUT OF THERE."
SO LONG,

BUT WHO WOULD WANT TO KILL ME?!

HA! HA! HA! HA!
HOHOHO! HEE!
HEE! HEE!
HA! HA! HA! HA!
HA! HA!
CHUCKLE
HA! HA!
HO!

OKAY, OKAY, SO I OWE A FEW PEOPLE SOME MONEY BUT--
OH MY GOD!

WHAT'S THE MAT--

OH MY GOD! ED!
COME ON! WE'VE GOT TO GET OUT OF HERE!

PANT PANT PANT I DON'T SEE HIM. WE MUST'VE LOST HIM.
LET'S NOT COUNT OUR HORTA BEFORE THEY'VE HATCHED.
SPACE CAB!!

HE PROBABLY KNOWS WHERE I LIVE SO WE'LL HAVE TO GO TO YOUR PLACE.
BUT IF HE'S ANYTHING LIKE THE OTHERS, WE WON'T HAVE MUCH TIME.
"THE OTHERS?" YOU'VE DONE THIS A LOT HAVEN'T YOU?
2187

WELL... I ONCE PASSED 2,000 CREDITS IN BAD CHECKS. IT WAS FOR COLLEGE.
Sigh GOING OUT WITH YOU CAN BE DESCRIBED MANY WAYS BUT "DULL" IS NOT ONE OF THEM.

SHERMAN'S ROOMMATES ARE NONE TOO PLEASED AT THE PAIR'S ARRIVAL...
SO YOU BROUGHT A FUGITIVE FROM A MURDEROUS BOUNTY HUNTER TO OUR HOME?

WELL, IT'S JUST UNTIL WE FIGURE OUT WHO HIRED HIM AND STRAIGHTEN THIS WHOLE THING OUT!
DON'T WORRY, JANE, I'LL PAY FOR ANY DAMAGE. YOU TAKE CHECKS, RIGHT?

BOOM!

WAIT! BEFORE YOU KILL ME I HAVE TO KNOW: WHO HIRED YOU?!

I THINK I CAN ANSWER THAT ONE "DOROTHY!"

FAZE!

UH-OH.

POPPIN' PLANETOIDS! SHE'S AN ANDROID!
SHE IS?!
UH, I MEAN, UH, I KNEW IT!
THAT'S RIGHT, MR. DAVIES...

I'M AFRAID YOU'VE ALL BEEN THE VICTIM OF A TERRIBLE HOAX.!
WHAT TH--?!

"YOU SEE, I CREATED THIS ROBOT TO HELP ME CATALOG MY MASSIVE PERSONAL LIBRARY -- OVER 39,000 VOLUMES -- ON PRAXIS-9. DESPITE MY MASSIVE PERSONAL FORTUNE -- OVER 2.8 TRILLION CREDITS -- I BUILT IT USING KNOCK OFF BOOTLEGGED SOFTWARE."

"HERE'S WHERE MY TROUBLES BEGAN."
ROBOTS FOR DUMMIES

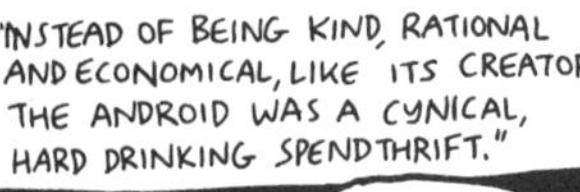

"INSTEAD OF BEING KIND, RATIONAL AND ECONOMICAL, LIKE ITS CREATOR, THE ANDROID WAS A CYNICAL, HARD DRINKING SPENDTHRIFT."

"LET THIS BE A LE
TO YOU ALL ABOUT
PERILS OF ILLEGAL
SOFTWARE."

SCREW YOU, EGGHEAD!

"BEFORE I COULD SHUT IT DOWN, IT RAN OFF. IT TOOK ME MONTHS TO TRACK IT DOWN."

JEEZ! I CAN'T BELIEVE I WAS HAVING SEX WITH A FREAKIN' ROBOT!!
I'M TERRIBLY SORRY, MR. DAVIES. SHE...
SHE MAY'VE BEEN A CHAINSMOKING, EVIL AUTOMATON, BUT SHE DID HAVE GOOD TASTE IN MEN FOLK.

HUH? WHAT DO YOU MEAN, GORGEOUS?
COME WITH ME TO PRAXIS-9, MR. DAVIES! HELP ME CATALOG MY BOOKS!

BUT WHAT ABOUT ME?!
NOW, LADIE
NOT BICKER! Y
BOTH HAVE M
MEANWHILE, BACK IN THE 20th CENTURY...
SWEETIE? I'M A LITTLE SHORT ON MY RENT THIS MONTH. CAN I BORROW...
END

BUSTER BROWNS
ICK!
by DINO! '99
BOO TOLD ME THAT SHE'D NEVER GO OUT WITH A MAN WHO WORE UGLY SHOES.

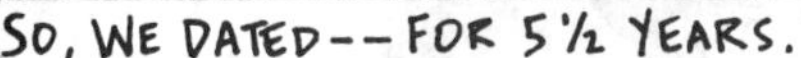
SO, WE DATED -- FOR 5 ½ YEARS.

YAY!

AND THEN... HIROSHIMA!
YOUR SHOES ARE...
...UGLY.

AFTER THE BLAST, I LIMPED ON OVER TO A FOXHOLE AND DREAMT THAT I PUT MY LAST DOLLAR DOWN ON LOTTO.

I WON SIX MILLION DOLLARS!
FIRST THING I DID WAS BUY EVERY PAIR OF GOOD SHOES IN THE WORLD AND THEN STORED THEM ALL IN A HUGE WAREHOUSE.
I PUT ON THE BEST PAIR OF THE BUNCH...
YOU'RE JUST NOT THE MAN I WANT TO SPEND THE REST OF MY LIFE WITH.
BOO WAS GOING TO HAVE TO DATE MEN FROM MARS, FROM NOW ON!

SMITH BROWN JONES:
ALIEN ACCOUNTANT IN
...AND NOW A WORD FROM OUR SPONSOR
CONSUME US CONSPICIOUSLY!
-Bean-
LANGUISHING, GROGGY WEASELS COMPEL ME.
I AM INVITED, BUT THE TABOO VOODOO BOO-BOO KEEPS ME AWAY.
I AM DISTURBED AND CAN'T BE IN A MEETING.
DACHSHUND.
WHY IS 7 FULL? 789.
THE LAZY SUSAN SPINS, OBLIVIOUS.

SHE IS GONE, ANON, REDEEMED... LIKE A VALUABLE COUPON.

ETRUSCAN! ETRUSCAN! REBAR! ETRUSCAN!

ALAS, ALACK, *SIGH*.

I AM UNDONE!

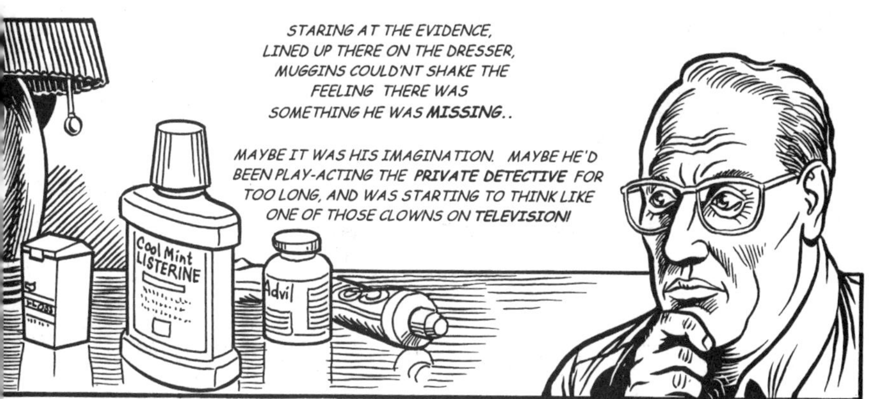

STARING AT THE EVIDENCE, LINED UP THERE ON THE DRESSER, MUGGINS COULD'NT SHAKE THE FEELING THERE WAS SOMETHING HE WAS **MISSING**..
MAYBE IT WAS HIS IMAGINATION. MAYBE HE'D BEEN PLAY-ACTING THE **PRIVATE DETECTIVE** FOR TOO LONG, AND WAS STARTING TO THINK LIKE ONE OF THOSE CLOWNS ON **TELEVISION!**
Cool Mint LISTERINE
Advil

...OR MAYBE IT WAS JUST THE **CLAUSTROPHOBIA** OF THIS TACKY OLD MOTEL ROOM...

BUT MUGGINS COULDN'T SHAKE THE FEELING THAT THE KEY TO **EVERYTHING** WAS RIGHT HERE IN FRONT OF HIM. **TAUNTING HIM**--
Advil
COLGATE

--TAUNTING HIM THE WAY THE WHOLE **CASE** HAD, EVER SINCE HE'D ROLLED INTO TOWN THIS MORNING...

THE KNOCK

A TRESPASSERS MYSTERY

BY JOE ZABEL

THERE IT IS— JUST LIKE I THOUGHT, THE ONLY MOTEL IN TOWN!
MMM... GOOD AFTERNOON! CARE FOR A ROOM?
YES, PLEASE, FOR TONIGHT.
I'D LIKE THE SAME ROOM HE HAD— DO YOU RECOGNIZE HIM?
I THINK SO— THAT'S MR. SAMARIN. ARE YOU WITH THE POLICE?
NO, I'M A PRIVATE INVESTIGATOR.
GEE, JUST LIKE MR. SAMARIN WAS!
COULD YOU DIRECT ME TO THE SHERIFF'S OFFICE?
C'MERE I'LL SHOW YOU. I HOPE THE SHERIFF MAKES YOU MORE WELCOME THAN HE WAS!

HOW LONG
YOU BEEN WAITING?
ABOUT AN HOUR.
THAT'S NOT BAD!
SOME FOLKS'VE BEEN WAITING
THEIR ENTIRE LIVES!
LEMME SEE YOUR
LEGITIMACIES...
THIS'S THE SECOND ONE OF THESE
I'VE SEEN THIS SUMMER.
THE FIRST ONE WAS SAMARIN'S.
AND NOW HE'S GONE MISSING.
SO YOU SAY. BUT THIS IS A
PEACEFUL, QUIET TOWN.
I'LL BELIEVE WE'VE GOT A
MURDER ON OUR HANDS
WHEN I SEE THE CORPSE!
YOU SAID THE SAME ABOUT FIELDING,
THE SAWMILL SALESMAN. HE SPENT ONE
NIGHT IN THIS TOWN— AND NEVER
SHOWED UP AT HIS NEXT STOP.
SO SAMARIN'S HIRED TO LOOK FOR HIM.
HE SPENDS THE DAY CANVASING YOUR
PEACEFUL, QUIET NEIGHBORHOODS--
THEN HE DROPS OFF THE FACE
OF THE EARTH TOO!
MORE'N LIKELY HE FOUND FIELDING—
OR FIELDING FOUND HIM!
BUT IT DIDN'T HAPPEN
IN THIS TOWN.
SAMARIN
COULDN'T 'VE WANDERED
TOO FAR AFIELD, SHERIFF—
HE WASN'T LIKE FIELDING—
HE LEFT HIS CAR BEHIND.
MAYBE SO. ANYWAY, YOU'LL BE
WANTING WHAT WAS FOUND OF
SAMARIN'S BELONGINGS IN
THE MOTEL ROOM.
DIDJA FIND
THE CAR KEYS?
NOPE.

LATER...

YOU TALKED TO HIM ABOUT FIELDINGS?
YEP.
WHAT'D YOU TELL HIM?
NOTHING MUCH. IT WAS JUST BUSINESS AS USUAL WITH FIELDINGS...

SAMARIN SENT AN EMAIL BACK TO US FROM HERE. DID YOU TALK TO HIM AT ALL, M'AM?
ONLY TO POINT OUT THE MACHINE TO HIM.

AFTER A LONG DAY...
WHAT'RE YOU HAVING?
BOURBON ON THE ROCKS.

I'M WITH THE FOREST CREST WEEKLY CHRONICLE. IS THAT GOOD FOR AN EXCLUSIVE ON YOUR MURDER INVESTIGATION
HMM! SURE.
SEVERAL DRINKS LATER...
...THE SHERIFF MOVES LIKE A GLACIER, BUT I TAKE HIS POINT— THIS TOWN'S GOT A THOUSAND SKELETONS IN ITS CLOSETS— BUT NOTHING CONNECTS WITH TWO STRANGERS WHO HAVEN'T SPEND A WEEKEND HERE BETWEEN 'EM...
HMMM...

AROUND 11 PM...

ICE
HONGS

YOU'RE SURE YOU HAVEN'T SEEN HIM?
NOPE. THAT'LL BE $13.85 WITH TAX.
12

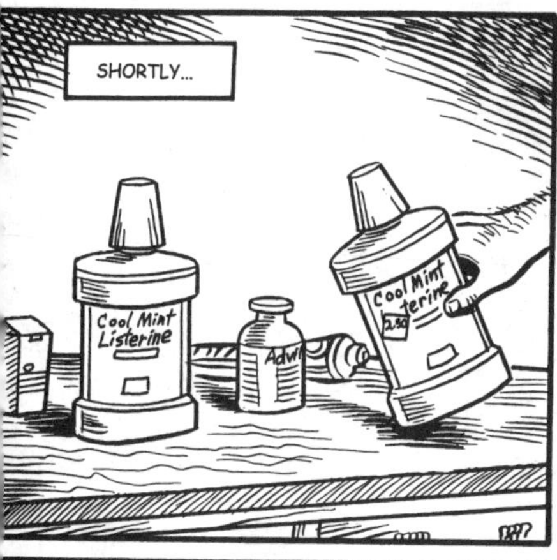
SHORTLY...
Cool Mint Listerine
Cool Mint Listerine
2.50
Advil

C'MON... SPEAK TO ME!
Advil
Advil

HMM... THE CAR KEYS— I HAD AN IDEA ABOUT THEM. OLD SAM DIDN'T LIKE TO LEAVE HIMSELF WIDE OPEN WHEN HE WAS TRAVELING. HE TOLD ME ABOUT A LITTLE TRICK.

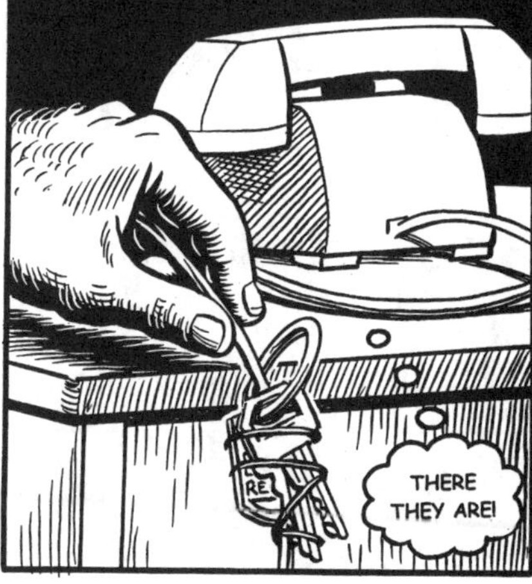
THERE THEY ARE!

KNOCK!
KNOCK!

KRUNCH!

LATER...

MANAGER

RING!

SORRY TO **BOTHER** YOU THIS TIME OF NIGHT--

THAT'S **ALRIGHT**, I'M ALWAYS UP— WHY DON'T YOU COME ON IN?

THINKING ABOUT THE **CASE**— I FEEL LIKE I GOT MY NAILS DER A **CORNER** OF SOMETHING, I CAN'T MANAGE TO PRY IT UP...

I THOUGHT A LITTLE **CONVERSATION** MIGHT HELP...

CONVERSATION? HA, HA, YES...

IT'S THE **PRICE TAGS**. WHY'D YOU **PEEL** THEM ALL OFF?

HUH?

I FIGURE IT'S BECAUSE YOU BOUGHT THOSE ITEMS AT THE LOCAL **QUIK-SHOP**. THE PRICE TAGS WOULD'VE BEEN A **DEAD GIVE-AWAY**...

HONEY, I DON'T FOLLOW YOU AT **ALL**...

BUT THAT LEADS TO THE QUESTION, Y'D YOU HAVE TO **REPLACE** THE ITEMS IN THE FIRST PLACE? WHAT'D YOU DO WITH THE **ORIGINALS**?

OH! **PIKE!** THERE YOU **ARE!** NOW MISTER, I'D ADVISE YOU NOT TO **MOVE**—

--OR MY BABY BROTHER PIKE IS GONNA **CRACK** YOUR SPINE LIKE A TWIG!

O-HO! YOU DON'T HAVE TO WORRY, M'AM. YOUR BROTHER AND I ARE OLD PALS! I GAVE HIM ALL THE CHANGE IN MY POCKET TO FEED THE COCA-COLA MACHINE, DIDN'T I PIKE?
PAT! PAT!
HUUGG! HEAH, HEAH!

YOU'RE NOT GONNA GET AWAY WITH THIS!!!

WHOA NOW! I THINK I'VE HEARD ENOUGH-- COME ON, SARAH YOU'RE UNDER...
YOWWWW!
THE NEXT DAY--
THE DISPATCHER SAYS YOU'VE FOUND FIELDING'S CAR.
YEP-- AND AT LEAST FIVE OTHERS! SEEMS SARAH WAS RUNNING A LITTLE CHOP-SHOP ON THE SIDE. THAT WAS JUST AN EXCUSE, THOUGH-- MAN-HATRED WAS HER REAL MOTIVE. FATHER-HATRED, PROBABLY.

I STILL CAN'T FIGURE WHY SHE HAD TO REPLACE THE STUFF IN THE MOTEL ROOM, THOUGH.
BECAUSE SHE'N HER BROTHER WERE BOTH HORDERS. WHEN SHE COULDN'T FIND SAMARIN'S KEYS, SHE HAD TO PUT EVERYTHING BACK LIKE IT WAS. BUT HER BROTHER'D ALREADY COLLECTED HIS SHARE--

SUPPOSE WE'D FOUND SAMARIN'S BELONGINGS COVERED WITH SALIVA AND TEETH-MARKS-- THAT WOULD'A LOOKED A LITTLE SUSPICIOUS!

IT'S ABSOLUTELY FREE. DO YOU HAVE ONE?

FANTAGRAPHICS BORING CATALOG AD #2 (collect all five!)

hurryhurryhurry!!come one come all!
COME ONE, COME ALL!
STEP RIGHT UP AND MEET THE WORLD'S MOST UPBEAT SUPER HERO...
Buzzboy!
I DON'T THINK THE "CARNY" GIMMICK IS WORKING, DOC.
NOT TO WORRY, M'BOY
I TOLD YOU THIS SMALL PRESS EXPO WAS A MISTAKE.
NO ONE HERE LIKES SUPER HEROES, BB...
Buzzboy
BECCA & DOC CYBER
AT
THE EXPO
BY JOHN GALLAGHER
THEY'RE INTO FANTASY, SELF EXAMINATION, IRONY...
I FEEL VERY SORRY FOR THIS GALLAGHER GUY...
SKY DOG
DON'T BE!

FUD
SUPER HEROES GOT NO BUSINESS AT SMALL PRESS SHOWS!
NO BUSINESS!
WHOA, DUDE! TAKE IT EASY!
SIR GARY GROTH SAID IT BEST! COMICS ARE DYING AND YOU AND THOSE OTHER DO-GOODERS ARE THE REASON WHY!
YEAH!
LISTEN, I LIKE THAT STUFF, TOO! THERE'S ROOM FOR ALL OF US...
NOOOOoo!
TRUE LIFE! SLICE OF LIFE! CHILDHOOD MEMORIES! TEENAGE SUICIDE! NONSENSICAL TALKING TOES! PEKAR! ZABEL! KOLCHALKA! NO ROOM FOR YOU!
HOLD IT!
LISTEN, INDY BOY! THERE'S PLENTY OF ROOM FOR SUPER HEROES, HORROR, HUMOR, SCIENCE FICTION-- WHATEVER!
AND ANOTHER THING!
FUD
COMICS IS THE ONLY MEDIUM IN WHICH THE SELF INDULGENT RAMBLINGS OF A MIDDLE CLASS WHITE MAN ARE STILL CONSIDERED AVANT GARDE! GROW UP! READ NORMAN MAILER!
COME BACK HERE!
PEREGRINE
INDY
FUD
I'M NOT THROUGH WITH YOU YET!
WOW! YOU WERE GREAT!
NAH! YOU'RE GREAT!
YOU'RE BOTH GREAT!
BUT DOES HE THINK SO?

DID SOMEONE SAY MY NAME?

MY UNIVERSAL TRANSLATOR CAN'T DECIPHER IT!

IT DOESN'T SOUND GOOD...

SEE, THIS IS JUST THE KIND OF DERIVATIVE GARBAGE THAT CONSTANTLY POLLUTES

WHO'S NORMAN MAILER?

FUD

LOOK OUT!

I THINK SOMEBODY JUST DISSED HIS PORTFOLIO!

HE LOOKS MAD. AN OLD ENEMY OF YOURS?

NOPE.

ANY LUCK WITH THE TRANSLATOR, DOC?

SORT OF...

EITHER HE'S HERE TO EAT YOUR TRASH...

...OR HE'S GONNA KICK YOUR
SHUT YOUR MOUTH!
...JUS' TALKIN' 'BOUT BUZZBOY...

BZZZBOY!
YIKES!
I BE SCARED!
DARN TRANSLATOR!
WELL, USE THE BUZZBELT!
NSIGHT
POWER UP!
YOU ARE SOOOO BUSTED!
BZZZBOY!
WAIT!
"...I'M YOUR BIGGEST FAN!"
SMALL PRESS
AUTO GRAPH ALBUM
...THE TRANSLATOR WORKS!
HE SAID...
Best Wishes!
-BUZZBOY
END

GEE, MISTER. I'M WRITING THIS BOOK REPORT FOR CLASS TOMORROW BUT I'M AFRAID TO USE ANY ORIGINAL IDEAS BECAUSE I DON'T THINK MY TEACHER WILL LIKE THEM.

NO MATTER HOW PURELY I DISTILLED THE VISION THAT BURNED IN MY BRAIN, IT NEVER QUITE MEASURED UP TO THE EVER-CHANGING VALUES OF CLIQUES AND CABALS I WAS SO DESPERATE TO IMPRESS.

IT WASN'T UNTIL I SQUELCHED THAT INNER VOICE; UNTIL I LEARNED TO TAKE ADVICE FROM MY MORAL AND INTELLECTUAL INFERIORS; UNTIL I CAME TO DEPEND ON THE PETTY MATERIAL COMFORTS THEIR APPROBATION MADE POSSIBLE; THAT I FOUND TRUE CONTENTMENT.

NOW, INSTEAD OF LOOKING BACK AT ALL MY FAILURES, I CAN LOOK FORWARD IN ANTICIPATION OF THE RELEASE THAT DEATH WILL BRING.

THANKS, MISTE I KNEW YOU' CHEER ME UP NOW, LET'S G GET A SLICE AUNT MAR CHERRY PIE

TAP TAP TAP
PTUI!
SNAP!
TAP TAP TAP
WIGGLE!
OOOHH!...
BOING

EVER SINCE I ACCIDENTALLY FELL THROUGH THAT INTER-DIMENSIONAL PORTAL AND DISCOVERED THAT MAGIC IS REAL...
...THE WORLD I WAS BORN IN HAS BEEN FOREVER CHANGED...
...AND IT'S PROBABLY BROKEN BEYOND REPAIR.
The Dreams of
Jax Epoch
from
Quicken Forbidden™
BY DAVE ROMAN AND JOHN GREEN
BECAUSE LATELY I'VE BEEN HAVING THE STRANGEST DREAMS...
LAST WEEK I DREAMT I WAS IN CLASS AND HAD A TEST TO TAKE, AND WHEN I WENT TO ANSWER THE QUESTIONS...
...I SOMEHOW FIGURED OUT IT WASN'T REAL...
...AND THEN INSTANTLY WOKE UP.
IT WAS JUST A DREAM?
MY ROBOT FRIEND A.M. WAS THERE ASKING IF I WANTED ANY COFFEE...
"THE BEST PART OF WAKING UP..."
I'M EXHAUSTED. I JUST WANT TO STAY IN BED.

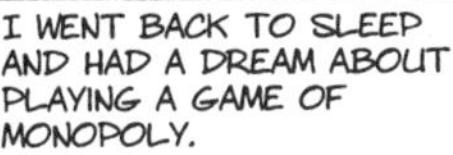
I WENT BACK TO SLEEP AND HAD A DREAM ABOUT PLAYING A GAME OF MONOPOLY.

THIS IS CALLED CALIFORNIA MONOPOLY...

...EVERY 15 MINUTES YOU HAVE TO SHAKE THE BOARD TO SIMULATE EARTHQUAKES.
I CAN'T REMEMBER IF I WON OR NOT.

I JUST REMEMBER THAT I WAS THE TOP HAT AND THAT THERE WERE TWO CARDS FOR PARK PLACE.
MAYBE ONE'S FOR SOUTH AND ONE'S FOR WEST?

THEN MY ALARM CLOCK WENT OFF...
...AND I REALIZED I WAS ACTUALLY STILL IN BED, NOT PLAYING MONOPOLY.

I THOUGHT ABOUT GOING OUT FOR SOME BAGELS WHEN SUDDENLY, MY BED GREW TWENTY FEET IN SIZE!

LUCKILY, THE BAGEL SHOP WASN'T TOO FAR AWAY.
STOP, YOU ALMOST PASSED IT.

I MADE SURE TO LEAVE PLENTY OF CRUMBS FOR THE PILLOWS AND SHEETS TO NIBBLE ON.

AFTERWARDS, I GOT DRESSED AND HAD A LONG DAY OF TRYING TO FIGURE OUT MAGIC SPELLS.

I'M POOPED.
WHEN I FELL ASLEEP I IMAGINED MYSELF PUTTING ALL MY LOOSE CHANGE INTO COIN WRAPPERS...
$1 PENNIES $1
$5 QUARTERS $5
...LABELING ALL MY SOCKS WITH A BLACK MAGIC MARKER...
...FIGURING OUT MY TAXES...
DE... DUC... TION...
...AND WATCHING BOWLING ON TV.
YES! GUTTER BALL!
I WAS SWIFTLY AWOKEN WHEN CRASHING INTO MY ROOM CAME A GIANT MECHA-SUIT...
...WORN BY AN EVIL TURTLE.

I WAS LUCKY I HAD PRACTICED THOSE SPELLS EARLIER IN THE DAY...

...AND WAS ABLE TO RECITE THEM FRESH FROM MEMORY.

POP!

HERE, KID. WANT A PET TURTLE?
DRATS! I UNDERESTIMATED HER POWER!
DOES HE COME WITH THE ROBOT?

SORRY, THIS IS GOING IN MY PERSONAL COLLECTION.

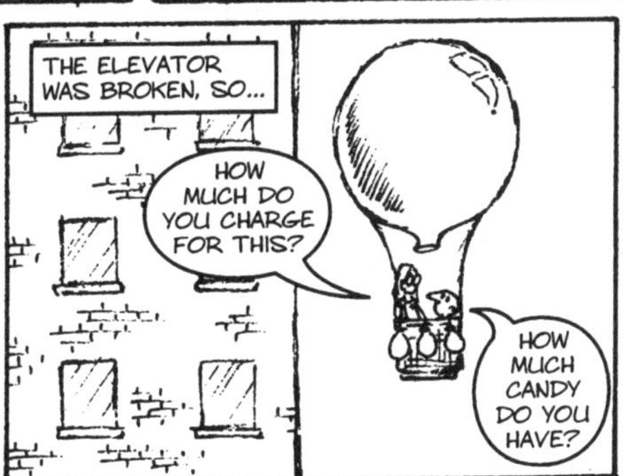
THE ELEVATOR WAS BROKEN, SO...
HOW MUCH DO YOU CHARGE FOR THIS?
HOW MUCH CANDY DO YOU HAVE?

MEET YOUR NEW FRIENDS.

AND AFTER ALL THAT, I DIDN'T DREAM AT ALL...
The End

3 FINGER PRINTS
PRESENTS:
THE 3 GEEKS IN
WHO THE HECK IS THE CBLDF?
STORY & ART by RICH KOSLOWSKI
SPECIAL GUEST APPEARANCES BY: CHRIS OARR & JAMES KOCHALKA, ☆SUPERSTAR☆
AHH, THE SMALL PRESS EXPO! A CORNUCOPIA OF TODAYS FINEST INDEPENDANTLY CREATED COMIC BOOKS. 'TIS A MAGNIFICENT DAY TO BE ALIVE COMRADES! TRULY MAGNIFICENT!
GREATEST COMICS
TEE HEE OH BOY OH BOY!
LET OUR GLORIOUS ADVENTURE BEGIN ENOW!
I.B.
1

HELLO GENTLEMEN!
COME ON OVER AND CHECK OUT THE CBLDF BOOTH.
CBLDF
WE'VE GOT ALOT OF GREAT STUFF THIS YEAR.
BULL

AND, OF COURSE, ALL PROCEEDS GO DIRECTLY TO THE CBLDF.
BULK

?

ER..... WHO'S SEEBEE-ELDEE-EF?
SOME NEW VILLAIN?

WELL NOW, THAT'S A FAIR QUESTION.

2

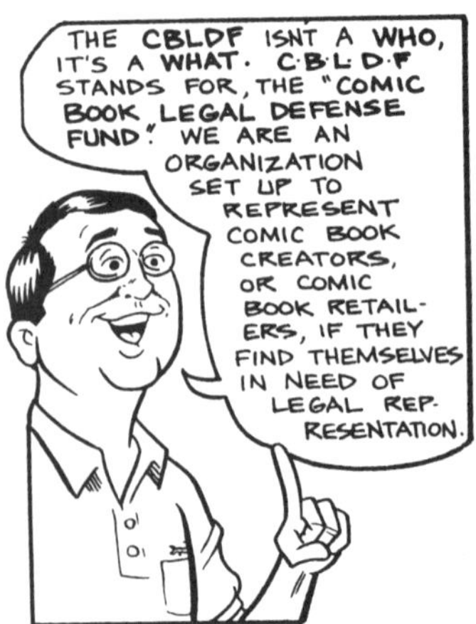
THE CBLDF ISN'T A WHO, IT'S A WHAT. C·B·L·D·F STANDS FOR, THE "COMIC BOOK LEGAL DEFENSE FUND." WE ARE AN ORGANIZATION SET UP TO REPRESENT COMIC BOOK CREATORS, OR COMIC BOOK RETAILERS, IF THEY FIND THEMSELVES IN NEED OF LEGAL REPRESENTATION.

IT'S A GREAT CAUSE, AND YOU NEVER KNOW, SOMEDAY ONE OF YOU MAY WORK IN THE FIELD, AND NEED LEGAL REPRESENTATION, •HEH HEH•
COMIC
BULK

SO, YOU SAYIN' THAT IF SOME DUDE, LIKE, STOLE MY COMICS AN' I STUCK MY SHIV 'TWEEN HIS RIBS, YOU'D DEFEND ME?

WHA...?
UH....
NO.

WOULDST THOU REPRESENT ME IF I FILED A GRIEVANCE 'GAINST MINE LOCAL SHOPKEEPER? RECENTLY, I DIDST RECEIVE A COPY OF THE LATEST "INHUMANES" AND THE UPPER RIGHT CORNER WAS SLIGHTLY CREASED!
SURELY HE MUST PAY FOR HIS INDISCRETION.

UM...NO. AGAIN, THAT'S... UH... NOT SOMETHING WE WOULD HANDLE.
BULK

3

OOH! OOOH! OOH! IVE GOT ONE! I HEARD THAT SOME BRANDS OF COMIC BOOK BAGS HAVE BEEN DETERIORATING OVER LONG PERIODS OF TIME. AND THE DETER-IORATION IS CAUSING DAMAGE TO THE COMIC BOOKS INSIDE.

I BET THAT WE COULD SUE THE MANUFACTURERS OF THOSE BAGS FOR TONS OF MONEY!
I MEAN, THE EMOTIONAL TRAUMA ALONE'S GOTTA BE WORTH MILLIONS!

NO, NO, NO. YOU DON'T UNDERSTAND. THAT'S NOT WHAT WE'RE HERE FOR.
LET ME TRY TO EXPLAIN...

WHAT!? YOU SAYIN' WE AIN'T GOT GOOD ENOUGH CASES FER YA!?!

NO! I'M NOT SAYING THAT AT ALL... WELL, YES I AM BUT.... YOU JUST DON'T UNDERSTAND. WE DON'T...
HM....

...LET ME SEE IF I CAN EXPLAIN THIS BETTER....

4

IM TRYING TO THINK OF A GOOD EXAMPLE...

HEY LITTLE GIRL DO YOU LIKE PONIES? WOULD YOU LIKE A PONY RIDE? I KNOW A PONY AND HE'S FRIENDLY, HE'D LIKE TO GIVE YOU A RIDE.

GIDDYUP LITTLE PONY
PONY THE PENIS!!

INTRODUCE MY PONY TO YOUR VENUS!
MR. MICROPHONE
CDLD
BULK

GIDDYUP LITTLE PONY
PONY THE PENIS.....

NOW THERE IS A GOOD EXAMPLE.
END

5

WRITTEN AND EXPERIENCED BY CHRIS BLEISTEIN
DRAWN AND ENVIED BY CHRIS SHADOIAN ~ YOW!
THIS LITTLE PIGGY
THERE'S ONE THING I'LL ALWAYS REMEMBER ABOUT MY KINDERGARTEN TEACHER, MISS COKE...
"PIGGY"

SURE, SHE WAS BEAUTIFUL, WITH LEGS LONGER THAN ME. AND SHE LIKED SHORT, LOOSE SKIRTS. SHE'D PERCH ON THE EDGE OF HER DESK WHILE TALKING TO US OR TELLING US STORIES.
MARKET
I HAD THE ALPHABETICAL ADVANTAGE OF SITTING UP CLOSE.
OFTEN, SHE'D KICK OFF HER SANDALS AND REST HER FEET ON MY DESK.
I DIDN'T MIND.
28
SOMETIMES, ON QUIET DAYS, SHE'D TAKE THE LIBERTY OF PAINTING HER TOENAILS WHILE SHE TALKED.
HOME

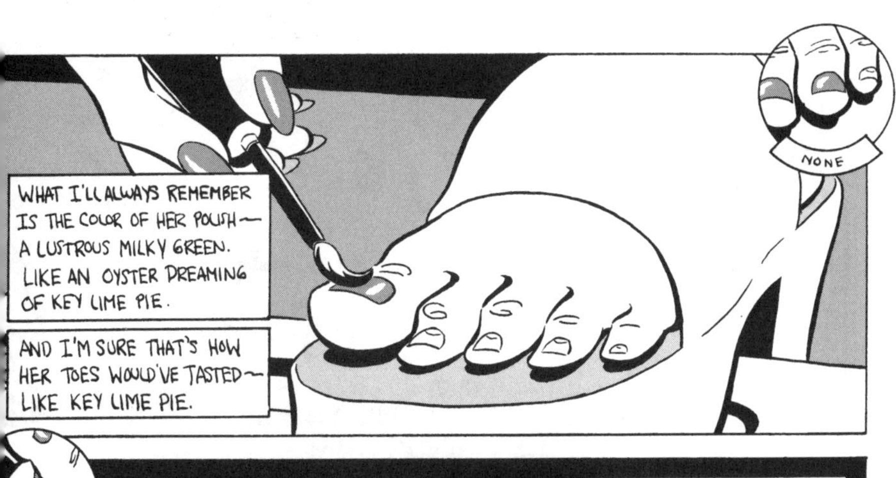

WEE
I CAN'T RECALL ANY OF MY CLASSMATES.
I DON'T REMEMBER WHAT OUR LESSONS WERE.
WEE!
WEE!!
I HAD MORE IMPORTANT THINGS TO LEARN.
WOW... I DIDN'T KNOW THEY MADE **FUR** PANTIES!

TRUE STORY, FOLKS! THE UNBELIEVABLE PART IS I DIDN'T END UP WITH A FOOT FETISH!
THE NAPE OF THE NECK...
...OR A NICE NAVEL...
...CAN CARRY MORE EROTIC CHARGE THAN TEN TOES TOGETHER.
PALE GREEN NAIL POLISH, ON THE OTHER HAND (OR WHEREVER), IS ANOTHER STORY...

yet another prelude tale of
the fire breathing
Pope TM©
I.N.R.I.
adapted freely from an ancient catholic joke. -author unknown. this version TM©
CHRIS YAMBAR 1999

ANY YEARS AGO, A YOUNG PRIEST WANTED
MAKE SOME MONEY TO HELP THE NEEDY
HIS CHURCH. HE WAS TOLD THERE WAS
FORTUNE TO BE MADE IN HORSE RACING,
O HE DECIDED TO BUY A RACE HORSE. AT
HE AUCTION, HOWEVER, THE PRICES FOR
ACE HORSES WERE WAY TOO STEEP, SO
E PURCHASED A DONKEY INSTEAD.

WHEN HE ENTERED THE DONKEY IN THE RACE, EVERYONE LAUGHED AT HIM. TO EVERYONE'S SURPRISE THE LITTLE DONKEY CAME IN THIRD PLACE. IT WAS A REAL MIRACLE INDEED.

HE NEXT DAY THE RACING SHEETS
ARRIED THE HEADLINES:
"PRIEST'S ASS SHOWS".

THIS ANGERED THE BISHOP VERY MUCH; SO IN ORDER TO STOP THAT SORT OF PUBLICITY, HE ORDERED THE YOUNG PRIEST NOT TO ENTER THE DONKEY IN ANY MORE RACES.

NO NO NO NO
NO NO
NO NO NO
NO NO NO
NO
NO
NO

THE NEXT DAY THE NEWSPAPER HEADLINES READ:
"BISHOP SCRATCHES PRIEST'S ASS."
KNOK KNOCK
Vatican NEWS

THIS WAS TOO MUCH FOR THE OLD BISHOP, SO HE ORDERED THE PRIEST TO GET RID OF THE DONKEY. THE PRIEST DECIDED TO GIVE THE LITTLE DONKEY TO A NUN IN A NEARBY ORPHANAGE.

THE VERY NEXT DAY THE PAPERS HEADLINES BOLDLY PRINTED:
"NUN HAS BEST ASS IN TOWN."

THE BISHOP NEARLY FAINTED. HE FIRMLY COMMANDED THE NUN TO GET RID OF THE DONKEY ONCE AND FOR ALL. SHE QUICKLY SOLD IT TO A NEEDY FARMER FOR A MERE TEN DOLLARS.

THE NEXT DAY THE NEWSPAPER HEADLINE STATED:
"NUN PEDDLES ASS FOR TEN DOLLARS."

Vatican NEWS
NUN PEDDLES ASS FOR 10 DOLLARS!

THEY BURIED THE OLD BISHOP THE NEXT MORNING AT 10 A.M.

THE END

MR. BEAT!™
and his sidekick
PLATT™
examine the freedom of speech!©
by CHRIS YAMBAR — 1999
EVEN NOW SOME PEOPLE KEEP ON GETTING THINGS CONFUSED WHEN THE WORD 'RESPONSIBILITY' IS BROUGHT INTO CONJUNCTION WITH THE TERM — 'FREEDOM OF SPEECH'. IT SEEMS TO SCARE SOME PEOPLE TO DEATH!
SPX

WE LIVE IN A COUNTRY WHERE THE FREEDOM OF SPEECH (THE ABILITY TO EXPRESS IDEAS AND EMOTIONS WITHOUT ANY RESTRAINT) IS ALWAYS UNDER ATTACK BY THOSE WHO WISH TO SUBVERT IT'S POWER AND POTENTIAL FOR THEIR OWN PERSONAL GOALS AND AGENDAS. (SIP!)

THESE 'MUZZLERS' ALL ADVOCATE THE CENSORSHIP OF CERTAIN CONTENT AND ARTISTIC EXPRESSION CUZ THEY DON'T CONFORM TO THEIR UNDERSTANDING OF HOW THINGS SHOULD BE IN THIS WORLD. THIS ISN'T IMITED TO OUR FRIENDS ON THE RELIGIOUS RIGHT (WHY THEY GET ANY PRESS AT ALL IS BEYOND ME) BUT IS ALSO HELD BY OLITICIANS, ACTIVISTS, AND CERTAIN...

... ARTISTIC AND JOURNALISTIC THINK-TANKS AS WELL. ON ONE HAND THE 'MUZZLERS' WANT TO IMPOSE RESTRICTIONS TO THE FREEDOM, WHILE ON THE OTHER HAND 'UTOPIANS' WANT THE FREEDOM TO SAY OR DO ANYTHING THEY WANT WITHOUT ANY OPPOSITION, NEGATIVE REACTION, OR PERSONAL RESPONSIBILITY FOR THEIR STATEMENTS, STANDARDS, AND ACTIONS.

ACME

BOTH GROUPS TEND TO MISS THE GLARING FACT THAT THEY ARE VICTIMS OF A DEADLY DISEASE CALLED 'SOCIAL AND INTELLECTUAL ELITISM'. THIS TYPE OF ILLNESS AND BLINDNESS HARDENS THE EAR WHENEVER THE WORD 'RESPONSIBILITY' COMES INTO THE MATHEMATICS AND...

..IT KILLS ANY CHANCE OF A HEALTHY DISCOURSE TOWARD A MIDDLE-GROUND MEETING OF THE MINDS ON THE TOPIC AT HAND. NOW, SINCE I'M A FIRST AMENDMENT ABSOLUTIST, I NATURALLY WANT TO DO EVERYTHING IN MY POWER TO PRESERVE THE FREEDOMS I HAVE TO EXPRESS MYSELF AT ALL COST.

AND SO SHOULD YOU!
REALLY!

BUT — EVERYONE KNOWS THAT NO TWO PEOPLE ARE GOING TO AGREE ON EVERYTHING — WHETHER THEY'RE BOTH FIRST AMENDMENT ABSOLUTISTS OR NOT. THAT'S JUST A FACT OF LIFE! PEOPLE ARE ALL UNIQUE AND ARE PRECIOUS IN THEIR INDIVIDUALISM. THERE'S A NUGGET OF GOLD UNDER EACH MOUNTAIN.

FOR SOME THOUGH IT REQUIRES ALOT MORE DIGGING THAN FOR OTHERS. FACT NUMBER TWO: NOT EVERY HUMAN HAS USE OF BASIC 'COGNITIVE REASONING SKILLS'. IN SHORT, SOME PEOPLE ARE OPINIONATED IDIOTS WHO COULDN'T BE MOTIVATED BY LESS THAN A BOARD UPSIDE THE HEAD AT 60 MILES PER HOUR.

THIS COMES FROM A LACK OF QUALITY EDUCATION, A VOID OF COMMON HORSE SENSE, AND THE VALUING OF ONE'S OWN OPINION IN SPITE OF RESEARCHED FACT AND LOGIC. WE ALL KNOW DOZENS OF PEOPLE WHO ARE LIKE THIS.

SOMETIMES IN ORDER TO PRESERVE OUR FREEDOM OF SPEECH AND EXPRESSION, WE'VE GOT TO THINK AHEAD AND SET UP SOME GUIDELINES TO KEEP THINGS FLOWING IN A PROGRESSIVE MANNER FOR ALL SIDES.

HA! SO THIS HOMO SAYS TO THIS NUN...

HEY!

REACTIONARIE CALL ANY TYPE OF LABELING 'CENSORSHIP'

BOOT!

THEY FEEL THAT ANY STATEMENT OF CONTENT OR WARNING MAY BE AN INFRINGEMENT ON THEIR RIGHT TO CREATE.

WHERE THEY GET THIS IDEA IS BEYOND REASON AND IS TOO EMOTIONALLY CHARGED AND PARANOID. LISTEN! SOME FOLKS LOVE TO EAT CANNED VEGGIES AND FRUIT BUT CANNOT HAVE TOO MUCH SUGAR OR SODIUM IN THEIR DIETS CUZ IT DOES NOT AGREE WITH THEIR SYSTEM, DIG?!

AN APPROPRIATE CONTENTS LABEL LETS SHOPPERS SEE THE CANS INTERIOR WITHOUT HAVING TO OPEN IT AND RUN IT THROUGH A SERIES OF SCIENTIFIC TESTS TO SEE IF IT'S ALL RIGHT FOR THEIR STANDARD OF CONSUMPTION.

Y'KNOW, I CAN'T REMEMBER A SINGLE RIOT OVER THE SALT CONTENT IN CANNED CORN.

ALL I EVER RECALL SEEING IS SOMEONE PUTTING THE CAN BACK AN' PICKING ONE WITH CONTENT MORE SUITED TO THEIR PERSONAL TASTE AND NEEDS. FOOD FOR THOUGHT I'D SAY! (PUN IS INTENDED)

IF WE FIRST AMENDMENT ABSOLUTISTS TYPES WANT TO 'BEAT THE HEAT', WE SHOULD CONSIDER THIS OBJECT LESSON. AT LEAST THEN, IF THE THOUGHT POLICE SHOW UP AT OUR DOOR, WE'LL HAVE TWO LEGS TO STAND ON AND SOUND REASONING IN SPITE OF THEIR ANTICS.

WHEW! ALBERT EINSTEIN ONCE OBSERVED THAT "GREAT SPIRITS HAVE ALWAYS ENCOUNTERED VIOLENT OPPOSITION FROM MEDIOCRE MINDS." THE WEIGHT OF HIS WORDS GAIN MORE AND MORE GRAVITY EACH PASSING DAY!

SOME THINGS NEVER CHANGE! BUT EVERY ONCE IN A WHILE THEY DO. IT'S OUR JOB AS FREEDOM ENFORCERS TO PUT OUR SHOULDER TO THE WHEEL AND KEEP THE FREEDOM OF SPEECH 'ABSOLUTELY FREE'! THE BALL'S IN OUR COURT IF WE LOSE OUR RIGHTS IT WILL BE BECAUSE WE REALLY DIDN'T VALUE THEM AT ALL! (SELAH)

F YOU DON'T LIKE SOMETHING SOMEONE IS SAYING THEN GNORE IT. IF YOU DON'T LIKE SOMETHING ON TV THEN CHANGE THE CHANNEL. F YOU DON'T LIKE A CERTAIN RODUCT THEN DON'T KEEP BUYING IT. YOU HOLD THE DECIDING VOTE – FOR YOU!

OF COURSE – CREATING A BETTER PRODUCT TO OFFSET AN INFERIOR ONE ISN'T A BAD IDEA. IT TAKES A LOT MORE SKILL AND CONVICTION TO CREATE AN ALTERNATIVE THAN IT DOES TO SIT BACK AND COMPLAIN ABOUT AN EXISTING ONE. DO IT, BABE!
JPUSA

SO BASICALLY I CAN DO AND SAY WHATEVER I WANT-WHENEVER I WANT-TO WHOEVER I WANT- AND GET AWAY WITH IT?!

SIP!

IT'S YOUR LIFE. BE RESPONSIBLE WITH IT!
S'UP BABY?!! I'M A FREE... THINKER! HOW'Z ABOUT YOU LETTING ME DRESS YOU UP IN A DAISY DUCK OUTFIT AND GIVE YOU AN OLD FASHIONED HOT OIL SPANKIN'? BRUSH OR BARE HANDED – YOUR CHOICE!
WOOF!
WOOF!
WOOOF!
WOOOF!

POW!

OH WOW!
SO GETTING DECKED WAS A RESPONSIBLE ACT ON MY PART FOR WHAT I SAID, HUH?
IT'S A START.
WHATTA YOU MEAN?

HERE COMES HER 500 POUND BOYFRIEND.
EEP!–

REMEMBER: AN OUNCE OF PREVENTION IS BETTER THAN A 'POUNDING' OF CURE!
BAM
BAM
AM
AM
END.

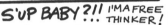

ris Yambar may be contacted by writing to: MORDAM COMICS, PO Box 1260, Youngstown OH 44501-1260 USA / calling (330) 799 1037 / or emailing him at: cyambar@hotmail.com

GREAT COMICS SHOPS

Supporting The Expo SPX99

BEYOND COMICS
GAITHERSBURG, MD
(301) 216-0007
www.beyondcomics.com

BIG BRAIN COMICS
DOWNTOWN MINNEAPOLIS, MN
(612) 338-4390
Our Bad Attitude Makes Us Better

BIG PLANET COMICS
BETHESDA, MD
(301) 654-6856
www.bigplanetcomics.com
The Comic Reader's Comic Shop

BIG PLANET COMICS
VIENNA, VA
(703) 242-9412
What He Said

CARDS, COMICS & COLLECTIBLES
REISTERSTOWN, MD
(410) 526-7410
Widest Selection In the Baltimore Area

CHICAGO COMICS
CHICAGO, IL
(773) 528-1989
www.chicagocomics.com
Chicago's Largest Selection of Alternative Comics

ONLY A MOVIE

JORDAN CRANE • 1999

THERE! YOU SEE HIM??
HE'S GOT THE GIRL!
lite

BAM
lite
git 'im!
BAM

AH BLEW HIM A NEW ONE.

NASS SHOOTIN'

... BUT... WHERE IS HE?

ROAR

EAT SILVER, VARMINT!!
BANG!
BANG!
BANG!

WHERE'S THE GIRL?
AH THINK AH SEE HER...

THERE, THERE.
YER ALL SAFE NOW.

THE END?

MOM?
DAD SEZ THE WEREWOLF'S NOT REAL CUZ HE'S JUST AN ACTOR WEARING FAKE HAIR 'AN TEETH 'AN SO HE DOESN'T EXIST – RIGHT?
SCENERY
SPECIAL EFF

MOM?

THAT'S RIGHT, TIMMY - AIN'T NO SUCH THING.

'AN NOBODY REALLY DIES - IT'S JUST MAKE-BELIEVE.
TOW
me

EVEN THE BLOOD'S FAKE.

JUS' FOOD COLOR & CORN SYRUP - IT'S ALLRIGHT, BOY.

JORDAN CRANE • 53 JOSEPHINE FLOOR No. 1 SOMERVILLE MA 02144
www.beat.com/jordan • jordan@beat.com

TITANS OF FINANCE

TRUE TALES OF MONEY & BUSINES[S]

SHE WAS SMART,
WELL-EDUCATED,
COSMOPOLITAN.
SHE WAS AMBITIOUS.
ALL KATRINA GARNETT NEEDED TO MAKE HER STARTUP A HIT WAS...

... A BRANDING EVENT.

L@@K THE PART*

BY R. WALKE[R] and JOSH'[S]

* Bibliography available: write for a copy.

KATRINA GARNETT FOUNDED **CROSSROADS SOFTWARE** PARTLY WITH HER OWN MONEY AND PARTLY WITH CASH FROM HER HUSBAND'S NEW VENTURE CAPITAL FUND.
SYBASE OPTIONS
ORACLE OPTIONS

SHE PULLED IN **HIGH-POWERED** INVESTORS...
I WANT TO FIT IN LIKE A MAN.
Dell Computer's Michael Dell
Armani

...AND CHANGED THE COMPANY NAME TO CROSS**WORLDS**. HER CONCEPT WAS "COMPETITIVE LINKING" SOFTWARE--
IF YOU **LOOK** THE PART, YOU **ARE** THE PART.
Wall Street heavy hitter Frank Quattrone

AFTER BEING IN THE DATABASE AND MIDDLEWARE SPAC... I COULD SEE THAT THE CUSTOMER... AS SHIFTING TOWARDS ... ATIONS.
WHICH SOUNDED--WELL, IT DIDN'T SOUND **SEXY** ENOUGH TO ATTRACT MUCH ATTENTION.

RICHARD AVEDON HELPED CHANGE THAT.
IS **THIS** BETTER, RICHARD?

THE FAUX-PROFILE ADVERTISEMENT APPEARED IN **VANITY FAIR, GEORGE, FORTUNE, THE ECONOMIST, FORBES, THE NEW YORKER,** AND **THE NEW YORK TIMES.**

PEOPLE NOTICED.

GARNETT DIDN'T SEEM CONCERNED ABOUT **CRITICS** WHO SUGGESTED SHE WAS "SENDING THE WRONG MESSAGE TO YOUNG WOMEN WHO WANT TO PURSUE CAREERS BASED ON THEIR **BRAINS**, AND **NOT** THEIR **BARBIE DOLL** BODIES."

COMPLAINTS, DEFENSES, EXAMINATIO **SATIRES** FOLLOWED. QUATTRONE QU THE BOARD OF DIRECTORS.

Junglee Corp CEO Rakesh Mathur

BUT IN EARLY 1999, GARNETT WAS SHRUGGING OFF THE CRITICS AND TALKING OF TAKING CROSSWORLDS PUBLIC.

I'M TRYING TO MAKE A **STATEMENT** THAT YOU DON'T HAVE TO COMPROMISE YOUR **FEMININITY.**
PEOPLE FEEL I'M A **GREAT** ROLE MODEL.

WE'LL SEE. MEANWHILE, HER **NOTORIETY** MAKES IT EASI TO DRAW ATTENTION TO HER CHARITABLE PROJECTS-- SUCH AS A **FOUNDATION** DESIGNED TO INTEREST GIRLS HIGH-TECH CAREERS...

EVEN IN **SILICON VALLEY,** GIRLS ARE CONCERNED ABOUT LOOKING **GEEKY.**

AND, IN FACT, THE **"SOFTWARE DIVA"** WAS RECOGNIZED FOR HER ACHIEVEMENTS NOT LONG AGO, WHEN SHE WAS NAMED...
... A **BARBIE AMBASSADOR OF DREAMS.**

BRUCE MUTARD

WHEN HITLER WAS AN ARTIST

*VIENNA

*VIENNA ACADEMY OF FINE ART.

Ahem... Herr Hitler.

Ja!
Oh... uh...
thank you.

Your folio please.
Oh... right.
Thank you.

mm... I hate the way they do that too. You'll never know what they might be saying about you behind that door.

They won't tell you when they call you in either. They're spineless cowards. They'll never tell you what they really think to your face - as though we're not men!

They're probably tearing strips off you in there - they think we're all morons.
I should know. This is the third time I've applied for this place.

Huhmph! I'll bet they take him. Anyone that young who applies must be something of a prodigy!

Hey kid, what's your name?

Hey, I said what's your name?
Uh... Egon.
Egon what?
Schiele.

here. Remember that Herr
tler. You'll be hearing more
it - say what is your
irst name?
Adolf.

Right. I'll remember that. Adolf Hitler. I'll reckon on hearing that again one day... mine's Reinhold--
Herr Hitler. Step in please.

Ach... well then my friend, this is it for you. Good luck and chin up! Confront the bastards. Don't let them step on you.

mumble...
mutter
mumbl...

....mutter...

Urm... Hk-kmm!
Herr Hitler.
Ja!

Tell us, why do you wish to come to this academy?

Er... Uhm... Well...

I er... have aspirations to become a painter... obviously, and... this academy is one of the finest training grounds for artists in Europe, so...

naturally I only want to learn from the best teachers in order to fully realize my ambitions in this field.

I greatly admire the work of Makart and David as well as Herr Griepenkerl who teaches at this great instit--
Yes, Yes, we understand your enthusiasm Herr Hitler - quite so. But...

there is the matter of your ability in question here.

Simply put Herr Hitler, we don't think your work betrays evidence of any natural gifts which we could refine into a full-fledged artist.

hilst you show some ommendable skill with andling pen and ink, e believe you lack the ye: the greater vision hat makes for a truly gifted artist.

Take for example this drawing here - a landscape near er... Linz isn't it? That is where you are from...

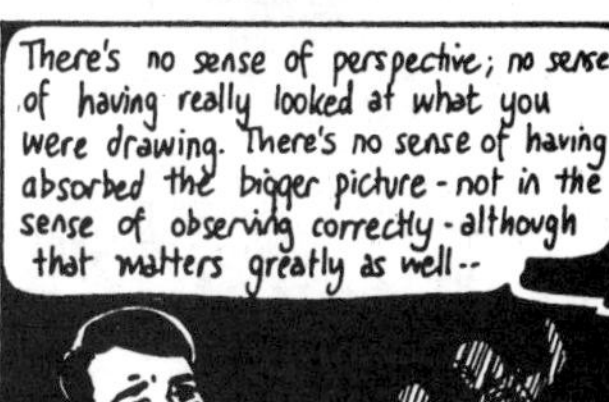
There's no sense of perspective; no sense of having really looked at what you were drawing. There's no sense of having absorbed the bigger picture - not in the sense of observing correctly - although that matters greatly as well--

but there's no personal vision. No vidence of your own artistic sensi ility coming through. That is what eperates the true artist from the erely skilful.

There are no drawings of the human figure here Herr Hitler. Why is that? The human figure is the central subject of art - we need to see evidence of your relationship to the human body.

We suggest you draw portraits of your family, your friends... go and copy some of the masterworks you admire in the Kunsthistoriches*...

* ART MUSEUM.

CLIC
CREAK

Herr Heinenger.
How did you go Adolf?

Oh... that good huh?
Ah well, too bad. You can try again next year.
Like I said, this is my third attempt and I'll wager that I'm still out.

Don't you worry my friend, you just keep at it. Teach yourself. Show the bastards they were wrong not to admit you.

I bet I'll be hearing your name again in the future: Adolf Hitler, the great artist of the twentieth century, and, he did it his way! You'll have this place grovelling to admit you as a teacher!

Say, why don't we meet later for a drink huh? What do you say?
Hey!
FIN

Beware the HORROR of...
Trick or Treat
Check out Dreaming City Tales volume 1 & 2 and keep your eye out for the first trade paper back collection coming this winter!
For more information contact us at Dreaming City Comics 5343 Essex Ct #51 Alexandria Virginia 22311 or E-mail Dreamkirk@aol.com
A DREAMING CITY PRODUCTION
STORY BY JIM KIRKLAND
PENCILS BY NATHAN MACDICKEN
INKED BY MARK A. W. JACKSON
FILMED IN SpookyVision
NR This story is rated Not Really a movie by the Motion Picture Assoc.
DREAMING CITY COMICS

The Cast:

Jim Kirkland as The Writer. Jim has worked in comic retail for over ten years and has been a fan of sequential art for much longer. He writes Dreaming City Tales and whatever else someone wants. He has many talented friends.

Nathan MacDicken as The Artist. Commercial and advertising illustrator for many years. Nathan's expanding list of comic credits includes sagas as The Tick: Heroes of the City and Vallator- Defender of the Future. Nathan is a student of the Force and plays the drums.

Mark A. W. Jackson as The Embellisher. A staple of the gaming industry, Mark's work graces projects from Wizards of the Coast and White Wolf Games. He claims he is currently teaching ebonics to the voices in his head.

NOBODY LIKES MISS FLETCHER.
BUTCH, YOU TAKE THAT DIRTY HAT OFF IN MY CLASSROOM.
SHE'S REALLY MEAN TO ALL THE KIDS, AND SHE REALLY HAS IT OUT FOR MY BEST PAL, BUTCH.
IS THAT A NOTE BEING PASSED IN MY CLASS?
SALEM, MASS
IT'S LIKE SHE HAS EYES IN THE BACK OF HER HEAD.
INSTEAD OF THE CREEPY ONE ON HER FACE.
YOU'LL BOTH BE SPENDING THE AFTER-NOON CLEAN-ING THE GUM OFF DESKS TODAY!
JUST LIKE HIS POPPA. TRASH BEGETS TRASH, BUT YOU COME FROM A GOOD FAMILY, MARTIN.
I EXPECT THESE KIND OF SHENANIGANS FROM TRASH LIKE BUTCH.

"YOU WATCH OUT OR YOU'LL END UP JUST LIKE HIM."
BOY, IS MY DAD GONNA BE PISSED.
I WAS SUPPOSED TO RAKE THE LAWN BEFORE HE GOT HOME.
TOMORROW'S HALLOWEEN. YOU GOING TRICK OR TREATIN'?
SURE, GONNA GET LOTS OF CANDY.
I'M GONNA SNEAK OUT LATE AND PRANK MISS FLETCHER'S HOUSE.
HOW? WE'LL GET CAUGHT!
NO WE WON'T! WE'LL GO REAL LATE. LIKE AROUND THREE!
I'M GONNA PUT DOG CRAP IN A BAG AND PUT IT ON HER PORCH.
LIGHT IT ON FIRE AND RING HER BELL. WHEN SHE COMES OUT SHE'LL STOMP ON IT TO PUT THE FIRE OUT!
THAT'S AN OLD ONE. SHE'LL KNOW IT WAS YOU.
NO WAY. ALL THE KIDS HATE HER. BESIDES, I OWE HER BIG.
WHERE THE HELL HAVE YOU BEEN!?! YOU GET IN HERE RIGHT NOW.
BUTCH'LL BE WALKING FUNNY TONIGHT. HIS DAD LOVES THAT BELT.

I'LL SEE YOU TONIGHT AT THE CORNER?
I DON'T KNOW. WHAT IF WE GET CAUGHT?
WE WON'T! COME ON, DON'T BE CHICKEN.
I'M NOT! I'LL BE THERE.
LATE THAT NIGHT...
LOOK AT THAT PUMPKIN!
WE'RE GONNA GET CAUGHT FOR SURE.

THIS WILL BLOW THAT PUMPKIN INSIDE OUT!
I'M STAYING HERE.
FINE. YOU EEP WATCH, CHICKEN.
AM NOT...
MARTIN TRIES TO WARN BUTCH, BUT HIS THROAT IS TIGHT AND NO SOUND EMERGES.

BUTCH IS GONE. IS HE DEAD? WHO CAN I TELL? WHO WOULD BELIEVE ME?
ADLER? BUTCH ADLER?
NOT HERE? PERHAPS HE HAD TOO MUCH EXCITEMENT LAST NIGHT?
HOW ABOUT YOU, MARTIN?
SHE KNOWS.
TO BE CONTINUED...

in

Shutterbug Follies

by Jason Little

Bee's new job allows her to make doubles (for her private collection) of all the photos she develops at Mulberry Photo.

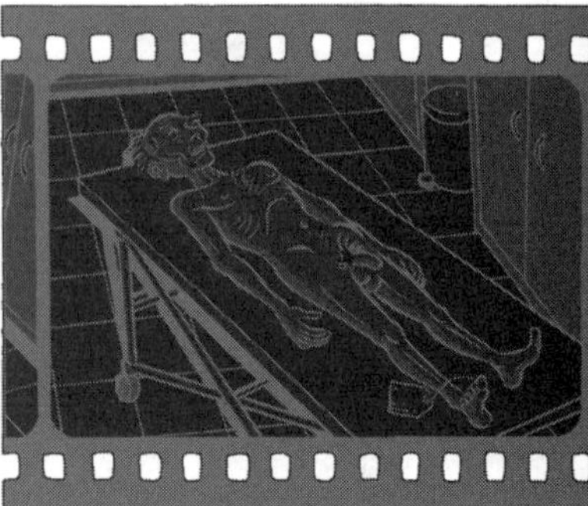

CHUNK!
C
M
Y
CLICK!

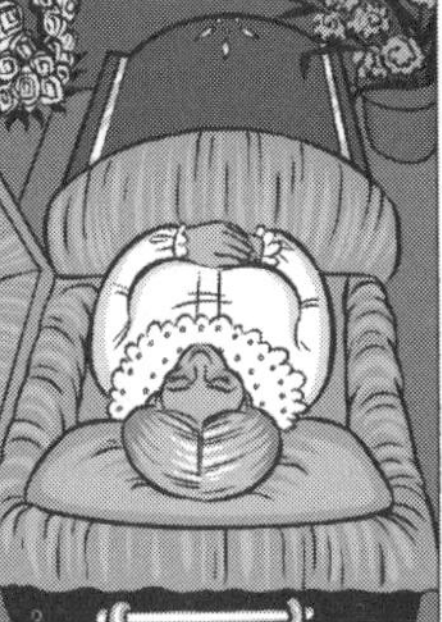

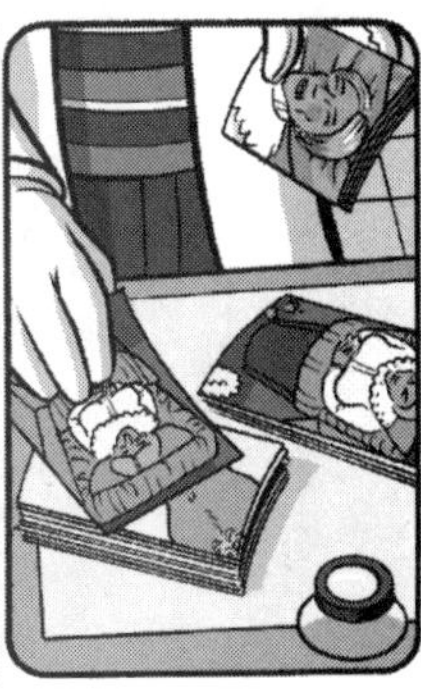

Hey, what do you make of this?
Oh, sorry, I should have warned you. He's a regular customer. Pretty creepy, mm?
Mm!

He fancies himself something of an artist.
Huh, really.

¡Ahem!¡
jingle

jingle

Hello! Are my latest preparations ready for scrutiny?

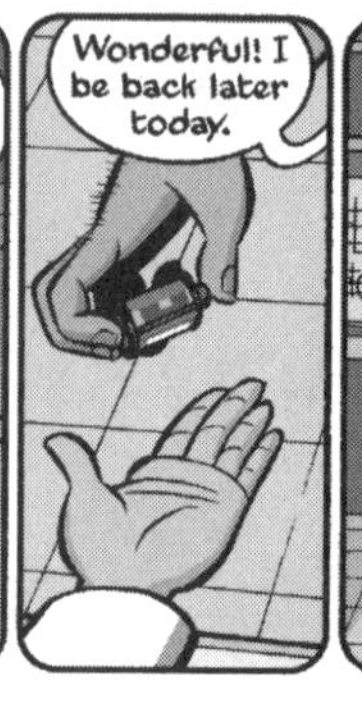

Watch Bee get caught up in a terrible mess when her adventur continue (in FULL COLOR) in your local alternative newsweek

city of BUTCH
TALES
stefan + clayton
© oats comic corp.
hair?
long ...brown...
he had big teeth
teeth?!
(they had hair on them)
o.k.
HOW OLD WAS HE?
40
So he was a 40 year old boy then?
yeah
thats right

people die on city streets.
† † † † † † †

fool Radz
clayton + stefan

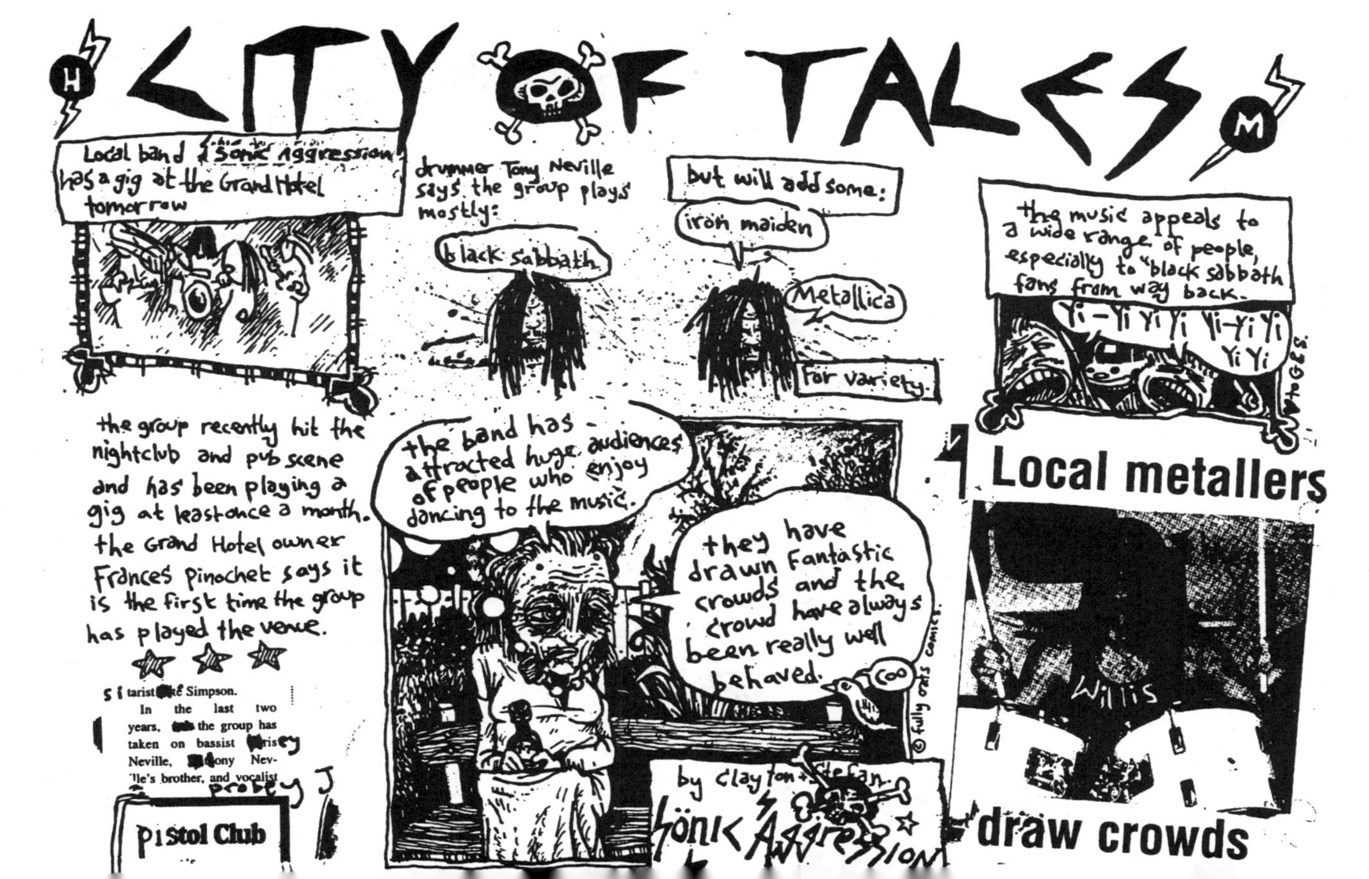

H
CITY OF TALES
M
Local band Sonic Aggression has a gig at the Grand Hotel tomorrow
drummer Tony Neville says the group plays mostly:
black sabbath
but will add some:
iron maiden
Metallica
for variety.
the music appeals to a wide range of people, especially to "black sabbath fans from way back.
Yi-Yi Yi Yi Yi-Yi Yi Yi Yi
the group recently hit the nightclub and pub scene and has been playing a gig at least once a month.
the Grand Hotel owner Frances Pinochet says it is the first time the group has played the venue.
the band has attracted huge audiences of people who enjoy dancing to the music.
they have drawn fantastic crowds and the crowd have always been really well behaved.
coo
© fully oats comics.
Local metallers draw crowds
Willis
tarist ke Simpson.
In the last two years, the group has taken on bassist Neville, Tony Neville's brother, and vocalist
Pistol Club
by Clayton + Stefan.
Sönic Aggression

WRITE: P.O. Box 1320, Dunedin, New Zealand EMAIL: yellow@es.co.nz

SINCE 1995, THIRTY THOUSAND PEOPLE HAVE MOVED HERE (MOST OF THEM WITH BAD HAIRCUTS).

WHERE'S THE CHICKS, BRA?

EEP!

PLEASE HELP!!!

THE APARTMENT VACANCY RATE IS AT AN ALL-TIME LOW OF ONE PERCENT...

WHAT'S THIS?

THIS IS TO GET ON THE WAITING LIST FOR PEOPLE'S COUCHES.

nerd

THE HOUSING CRISIS ALLOWS LANDLORDS TO BE AS GREEDY AS THEY WANNA BE...

I'LL PAY YOU A YEAR'S RENT UP FRONT PLUS A "BONUS" OF $2000, A NEW TV SET, THE USE OF MY SAILBOAT, SOME STOCK OPTIONS AND MY FIRST-BORN CHILD.

HMM, I ALREADY HAVE 5 BETTER OFFERS. COULDN'T YOU THROW IN AN ALL-EXPENSE PAID TRIP TO TAHITI?

34

THE MOST COMMON SCAM IS THE OWNER MOVE-IN EVICTION...
666
NOW I'LL MOVE MY SON IN FOR A COUPLE MONTHS AND THEN RERENT IT TO SOMEONE ELSE FOR TWICE AS MUCH!
20 YEAR RESIDENT
BLATANT LYING IS QUITE POPULAR TOO.
MY LANDLORD SAID SHE WAS SELLING THE HOUSE SO WE MOVED OUT. THEN SHE UPPED THE RENT AND FOUND NEW TENANTS.
SUDDENLY THE ONLY PEOPLE WHO CAN AFFORD THE SKYROCKETING RENTS ARE WHITE-COLLAR WORKERS...
Will Play Rad Solo For $$!
J. CHURCH
WHEN I FIRST MOVED HERE IN 1990, THIS TOWN SEEMED IDYLLIC.
A SAFE HAVEN WHERE ALL OF LIFE'S OUTCASTS, ODDBALLS AND REPROBATES WERE WELCOME...
I CALL IT "MOTHER."
MY ZINE'S GONNA BLOW THE LID OFF THE WHOLE McDONALD'S-ZOMBIE CONSPIRACY.
WOAH! PASS THE BONG AN BUTTPLUG

I'D GROWN UP IN A SMALL TOWN IN MASSACHUSETTS WHERE NOTHING EXCITING EVER HAPPENED...
WHERE CHINESE FOOD WAS CONSIDERED EXOTIC, WHERE CLOSE ENCOUNTERS WAS THE CLOSEST THING TO A FOREIGN FILM, WHERE CLASSIC ROCK REFUSED TO DIE...
YOU CAN'T REALLY COMPARE STYX TO BOSTON.
SAN FRANCISCO, ON THE OTHER HAND, WAS FULL OF INTERESTING PEOPLE. ANY NUT WHO COULD STRING TOGETHER A COUPLE HUNDRED COULD GET A ROOM.
ONE MORE SPERM DONATION AND LAB RESEARCH CHECK AND I'LL MAKE IT.
IT CERTAINLY LED TO SOME ODD ROOMMATES, LIKE THE SKINHEAD FOR PEACE WHO BEAT ON HIMSELF
CANNED VENISON
OR THE COMPUTER NERD PYROMANIAC WHO'D BEEN HUNTING IN ALASKA.
I WAS DISCOVERING WHOLE NEW WORLDS...
DUBLIN BESTED BELFAST LAS' NIT YA KNOW.
IRISH SPEED FREAKS
MUSIC NERDS
CHRIS MONTEZ
I LOVE THIS LP MORE THAN MY MOM!
TIGER TRAP
THIS'LL HURT YOU MORE THAN ME!
BAD BOY
DOMINATRICES

THEN THE INTERNET REVOLUTION HIT. SOON SILICON VALLEY YUPPIE SCUM WERE INFILTRATING EVERY CORNER OF THE CITY...
S.U.V.
CELLPHONE
COSMOS
ELBOW TIT
401(K)

GENTRIFICATION RAN RAMPANT...
PARDON ME SIR BUT YOUR BLOODY CARCASS IS BLOCKING MY CONDO ENTRYWAY.
GOLD-TIPPED LOAFERS

FANCY RESTAURANTS, THEME BARS AND STARBUCKS OUTLETS SPREAD LIKE A VIRUS...
LE CHIC
STARBUCKS COUGHEE
SMELLY DIAPER BAR
BON MERDE
BON MERDE
HIRING
COMING SOON: STARBUCKS
HIRING

RESISTANCE TO THE YUPPIE HORDE SPRANG UP IN TYPICAL CREATIVE SF FASHION...
MISSION YUPPIE ERADICATION PROJECT
THIS YUPPIE TAKEOVER CAN BE TURNED BACK. WE CAN DRIVE THESE CIGAR BAR CLOWNS BACK TO ORINDA.
VANDALIZE YUPPIE CARS:
BMWS PORSCHES JAGUARS SUVS
·BREAK THE GLASS
·SCRATCH THE PAINT
·SLASH THE TIRES
IF YUPPIE SCUM KNOW THEIR PRECIOUS CARS AREN'T SAFE THEY'LL GO AWAY AND THE TRENDOID RESTAURANTS, BARS AND SHOPS WILL GO WITH THEM.
-TAKE ACTION NOW!
IN CASE OF EARTHQUAKE GO BACK HOME
-the seismic solution
YOU'LL FINALLY GET TO USE YOUR 4-WHEEL DRIVE.
-SS
I'M COMING
BUT IT WAS TOO LITTLE, TOO LATE.

THE MAN MOST RESPONSIBLE FOR THE MALLING OF SAN FRANCISCO WAS "SLICK" WILLIE BROWN.
DO I GET PAID FOR THIS?
"DA MAYOR"

LIKE A LOT OF OTHER FOOLS, I VOTED FOR BROWN (EVEN AFTER DISCOVERING SOME DISTURBING NEWS)...
HOLY SMOKES! WILLIE BROWN FARTS WHILE HE PEES!
Blat!
Fzzt!

OF COURSE, THE CITY HAS A HISTORY OF STRANGE POLITICAL FIGURES AND EVENTS.
FORMER MAYOR FRANK JORDAN LOST RE-ELECTION PARTIALLY BECAUSE OF AN INTERVIEW HE GAVE IN THE NUDE.
FIXER JACK DAVIS NEARLY SUNK THE NINERS WITH A BIRTHDAY BASH THAT FEATURED A LEWDLY PLACED WHISKEY BOTTLE.
DAN WHITE KILLED HARVEY MILK AND MAYOR MOSCONE AND GOT OFF EASY WITH A BIZARRE DEFENSE.
MY CLIENT WAS NUTS FROM EATING TOO MANY TWINKIES.

BUT NEVER HAS A MAYOR SHOWED SUCH BLATANT DISREGARD FOR THE CITY, INTENT ONLY ON INCREASING HIS OWN POWER, WEALTH AND FAME...
STEALING PUBLIC ART FUNDS TO FINISH RENOVATION ON THE RIDICUOUSLY OSTENTATIOUS CITY HALL DOME.
YES!
YES!
YES!
STACKING THE BOARD OF SUPERVISORS WITH PRO-BUSINESS AND YES-PEOPLE WHO WOULD LOOK THE OTHER WAY WHEN HE MADE SECRET DEALS.
RAISING THE DEAD TO WIN APPROVAL OF THE 49ERS STADIUM DEAL.
MUST... VOTE... YES.
PAUL REVERE

EN

Published by Yields Under Gentle Pressure Press. 347 Divisadero Street, San Francisco CA 94117
EMAIL: brogrimm@pacbell.net

Interlude
by Gregory Cook
Copyright 1997

At 8 o'clock work

ends at the library and I

GLOUCESTER Sawyer Fr

NO Parki
walk to my ex-mother-in-law's to pick up

my daughter

and we head home.
Halfway home on Middle Street
there's this old white
REV. SAMUEL
CHANDLER
1752
51

barn of a house and at night there's

always piano music drifting down

to the street from a second floor window.

They give lessons there.

9·28·97

V stops and dances for a minute while I say
nothing and think of how my ex and I used to
pause here, holding hands, during our evening walks.
The End
thanks to Roctober!

BIG TROUBLE!

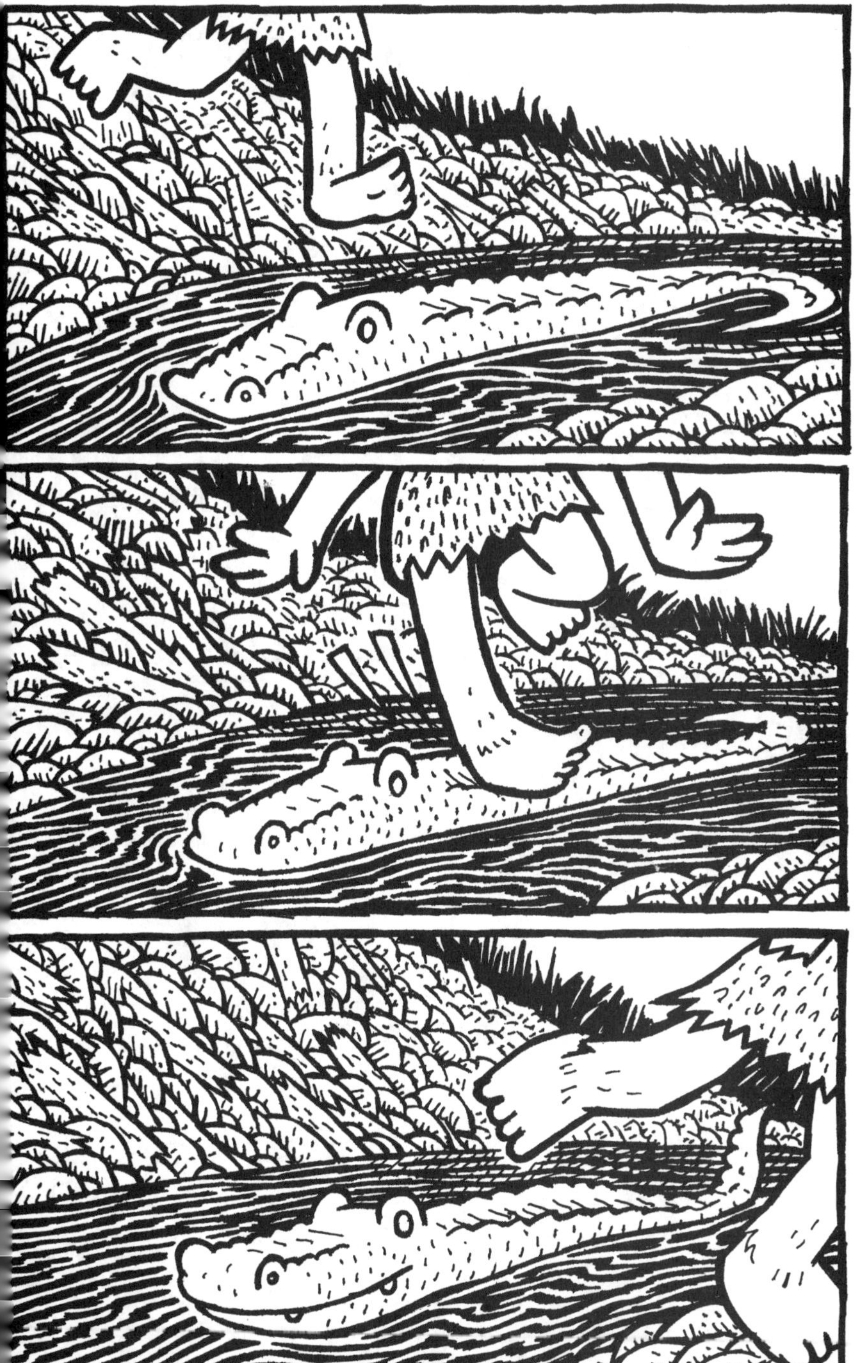

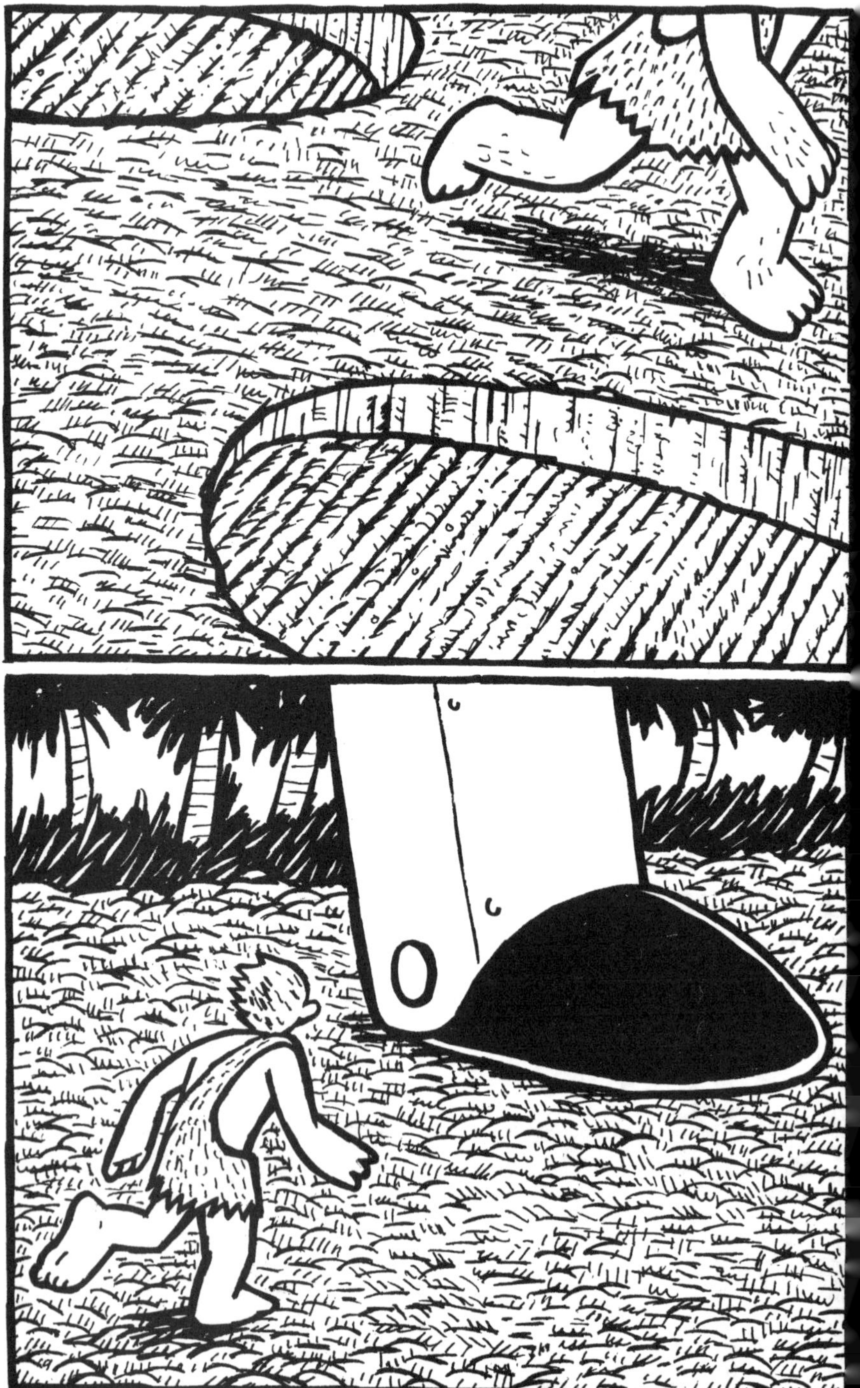

ZZ

ZZ

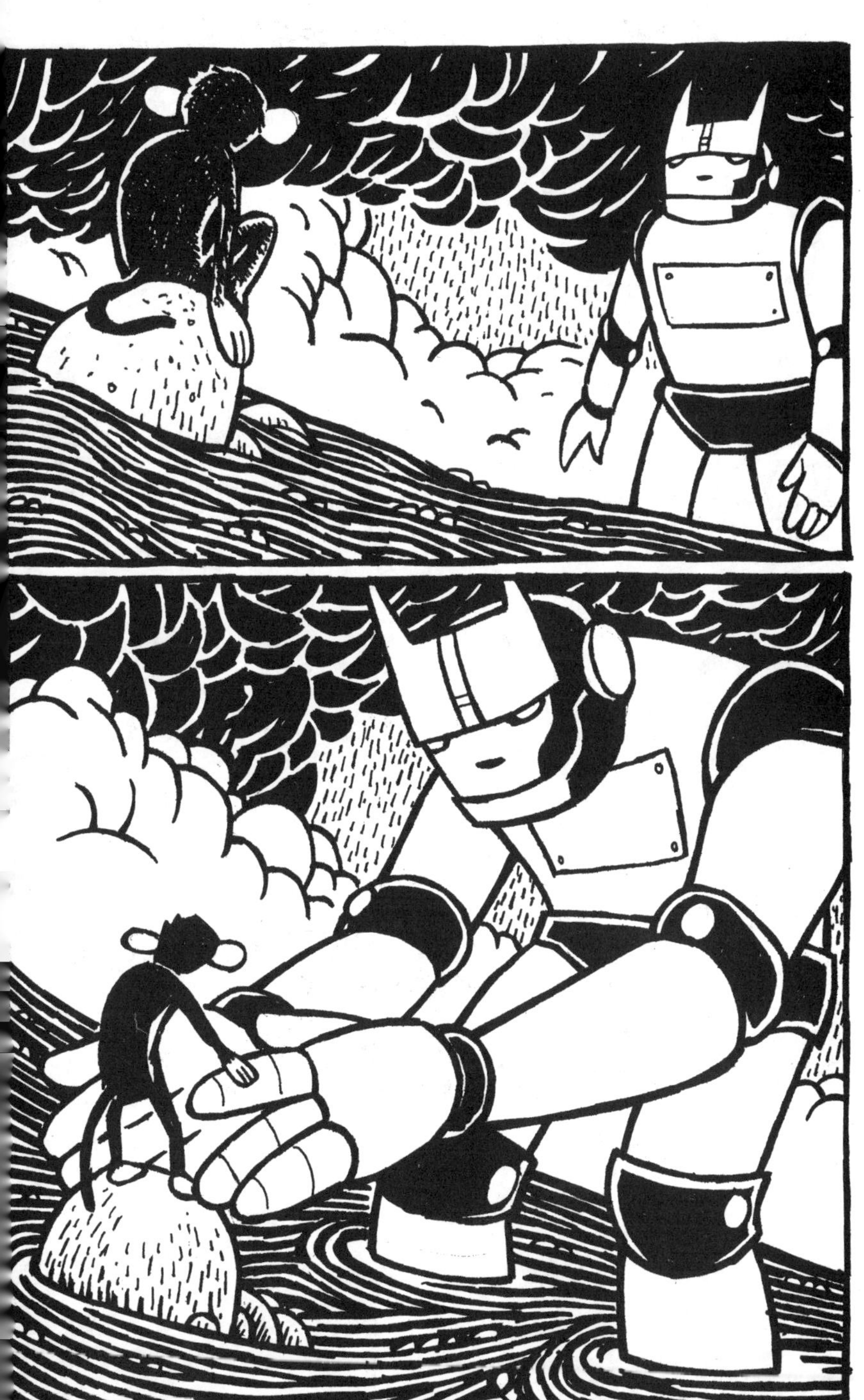

BRIAN RALPH

MERRY PEDROOLIA

IN WHICH THE CELEBRATED TRICKSTER PAU-HENOA MEETS HIS MATCH, IN A MANNER OF SPEAKING.
A GOREDDI FOLKTALE, ILLUSTRATED BY RACHEL HARTMAN

LONG AGO, IN THE FOOTHILLS OF GOREDD, THERE LIVED THREE BROTHERS AND THEIR LITTLE SISTER. HER NAME WAS PEDROOLIA.
NOW BEFORE YOU START SMIRKING, SMARTY, LET ME ASSURE YOU THAT OUR PEDROOLIA WAS AS LOVELY AND CHARMING AS ANY BLANCHE, MAUDE OR BLODWEN YOU'VE EVER SEEN.
SHE WAS, HOWEVER, A TAD ECCENTRIC. NO ONE HAD EVER SEEN HER SAD OR MAD EVEN TIRED. IF YOU ASKED HER ABOUT IT SHE'D JUST LAUGH, OR MAYBE SING.
Give me more chores That take me outdoors! I'd rather be feeding the sows + boars Than down on all fours Scrubbing floors...
SHE DROVE HER BROTHERS CRAZY WITH HER CHEER. I THINK IT'S FAIR TO CALL THEM HUMORLESS CLODS.
Humorless clods! Tee-hee!
You try living with her!
See how long it takes you to go mad.
GHEE! Make her stop smiling!

SHE CHUCKLED WHILE CHURNING BUTTER.
Churn-churn, chuckle-chuckle!
SHE JOKED WHILE SHEARING SHEEP.
A LEETLE OFF ZE TOP, MADAME? VERY GOOD.
MEHH
NO AMOUNT OF MANURE COULD KEEP HER FROM CUTTING CAPERS.
TRA-LA!
AND THEN THERE WAS THE MATTER OF BEING CHIPPER AT BREAKFAST...
Kippers! Kippers for everyone!
KLANG!
FINALLY HER BROTHERS COULD TAKE NO MORE.
What's this?
We're putting you in the coocoo house.
THEY PUT HER IN THE DOVECOTE AND LOCKED THE DOOR.
coo
I get it! Coo! coo! Ha-ha!
That's the first funny thing you guys ever said.
Uh... guys

A YEAR AND A DAY LATER, PAU-HENOA PASSED BY THEIR FARMSTEAD. THE PLACE WAS A WRECK— THE CROPS HAD WITHERED, THE SHEEP WERE SICK...
... AND FROM THE DOVECOTE CAME THE SOUND OF A WOMAN WEEPING.
IT WAS PLAIN SHE NEEDED HELP. TOO BAD SHE GOT THE MAD BUN INSTEAD.
Aw c'mon! Even I like to help the odd damsel in distress occasionally.
Emphasis on odd.
HELLOO DOWN THERE!
ARE YOU OKAY?!
No! My brothers left me here, and I'm beginning to suspect they're not coming back!
Would you say you're a damsel in distress?
Heh-heh.
I've been in DIS DRESS for a year, honey, and it ain't pretty.

PAU-HENOA WENT TO GET A LOOK AT THESE BROTHERS.
Should we do some work today?
Never liked work.
Never liked nothin'.
Just as I suspected!
Humorless clods!
SUDDENLY THE BROTHERS SAW A DASHING FIGURE COME ROUND THE SIDE OF THE HOUSE.
Greetings, yeomen. I am the count of Topo-el-Bumppo.
I wish to marry your sister.
Yeah, right, fancypants.
She's too valuab We won't give h up.
Not without a good bride-price, anyways.
Sigh! I owe all my wealth and prestige t my lucrative guano min but I would be willing t give it all up for... uh.. for whatshername...

For
Pedroolia?!
HAW-HAW!
SUCKER!
YESS!
A mine! WOW!
We'll be rich as fiends!
Mining's gotta be easier than farming!
Get up, sis. This fellow gave us a mine so's he could marry you.
I know you.
You do indeed.
Say, what IS guano, anyhow?
OOH! Brightness!
Heh!
Funny you should ask. Try living in it for a year.
Wha'?
Ew!
SLAM!

What a mess! This place needs a lot of work! Fortunately, I LIKE work!
What don't you like?
Oh, I'm not super fond of my brothers just now, but giv me time.
Help?
Please?
I can't imagine ever wantin another dove egg.
Come back in a year and we can let them out and see how they've changed.
YOU didn't change.
Ah, but you're wrong. I am much much graver than I was before, my eyes are open, and I have been seen in company with strange rabbit-men.
I'm an entirely different Pedroolia.
AND WITH THAT SHE SET TO WORK, SINGING. AND PAU-HENOA WENT HIS WAY, RESOLVING TO BE BACK TO COURT PEDROOLIA IN EARNES —FOR HE THOUGHT HER THE MOST CHARMIN AND CHEERFUL GIRL HE'D EVER MET, AND SHE WAS EVERY BIT AS ODD AS HE WA
I love the spring, I love the fall, I love my freedom Best of all...
All too rare a quality!

FORTY WINKS by Vince Sneed & Aaron McClellan
WAKE UP, PANDORA!
GOOD GRIEF, SAM! DON'T DO THAT!
I THOUGHT WE WERE SUPPOSED TO HAVE A PICNIC!
SO, WHAT'S ALL THIS?

I WAS THINKING ABOUT HOW I'D LOOK WHEN I BECOME A DREAM GUIDE LIKE YOU!
WHAT'S THE MATTER? DON'T YOU LIKE THE UNIFORM?
VERY COOL! I LIKE THE TRENCHCOAT.
I WANT SOME-THING WITH A LITTLE MORE *STYLE*. TAKE A LOOK!
THAT'S NOT ALL!
I'LL HAVE THESE LASER BEAMS THAT'LL SHOOT OUT OF MY FINGERS...
...AND BE ABLE TO MAKE A FORCE FIELD AND I'LL BE STRONG ENOUGH TO LIFT A TANK!
MORE THAN A MATCH FOR ANY OLD MONSTER!
YOU KNOW, DREAMS ARE PRETTY POWERFUL THINGS. THEY HAVE A WAY OF TAKING ON LIVES OF THEIR OWN!
HUH?
I'LL SH
YOU!
HELP!

huh
huh
huh
huh
huh
OHMIGOSH! I'M CONVENIENCE SIZED!
THIS IS TERRIBLE!
ALONE, CONVENIENCE SIZED, THE PERFECT DISH FOR ANY HUNGRY BIRD THAT MIGHT FLY BY AND SPOT ME! I'M DOOMED!
YAAAAAAAAAAAAAAHHH!
WAIT A MINUTE!
I JUST REMEMBERED SOMETHING!
I'M SUPER POWERED!

I'M A FORCE FOR GOOD, SO QUITE YER SQUAWKING, BIRDY!

NO TIME TO TEST MY FLYING ABILITIES, AND I'VE GOT INJUSTICES TO RIGHT, PRONTO!

IT JUST GETS BETTER AND BETTER, JAMIE!
THIS IS DEFINITELY THE BEST OF THE THREE!
WHAT? ARE YOU RETARDED? YOU THINK THIS IS BETTER THAN "EMPIRE"?!
TOTALLY!
WHY IN YODA'S NAME WOULD YOU SAY THAT?
WELL... THE EWOKS ARE COOL.
WHAT?! THEY'RE THE WORST PART OF AN OTHERWISE PERFECT MOVIE, MIKE!
HOW COULD YOU SAY THAT? THEY'RE JUST SO CUTE! AND, LIKE, "EMPIRE" DIDN'T HAVE A GOOD ENDING!
BUT AT LEAST THEY HAVE SOLO IN THIS MOVIE!
AND HE AND LEIA FINALLY GET TOGETHER!
YEAH, AND I LIKED HOW VADER KILLS THE EMPEROR!
I STILL CAN'T BELIEVE LEIA IS LUKE'S SISTER!
UM... EXCUSE ME, BUT WE HAVEN'T SEEN THE MOVIE YET.
REALLY? YOU'RE GONNA LOVE IT!
AND THE SPECIAL EFFECTS ARE, LIKE, AWESOME! THEY'RE NEVER GONNA GET ANY BETTER THAN THIS!
SIGH
I HOPE THAT KID WITH THE "NEW WAVE" HAIR DOESN'T SIT IN FRONT OF US. THAT'LL **REALLY** SPOIL THE MOVIE.

IT WAS 1983

"THE SUMMER OF THE JEDI"

I REMEMBER IT WELL

ALL 22 SCREENINGS
AND ESPECIALLY THAT ONE TIME...

I WAS 13 AND FINALLY ALLOWED TO GO TO THE MOVIES WITHOUT MOM HAVING TO DRIVE ME
I WAS EVEN ALLOWED TO TAKE THE BUS DOWNTOWN IF AT LEAST TWO OF THE MIKES WERE WITH ME
TO THIS DAY, I DON'T UNDERSTAND MOM'S "YOU SHOULD AT LEAST TRAVEL IN THREES WHEN YOU'RE DOWNTOWN" THING
ANYWAY, I TOOK FULL ADVANTAGE OF MY NEW-FOUND FREEDOM THAT SUMMER...
MAY I SEE YOUR TICKETS, PLEASE?
I REMEMBER SEEING A LOT OF MOVIES
ALL DOWNTOWN... EVEN THOUGH SOME FILMS WERE PLAYING AT THEATRES A TEN-MINUTE WALK FROM MY HOUSE
WE MAY HAVE EVEN SNUCK INTO ONE OR TWO...
YOU WANTED TO USE YOUR "COOL POCKETS," REMEMBER?
"THE FORCE IS STRONG IN MY FAMILY."
... I DON'T HAVE THEM...
PLEASE COME WITH ME TO THE MANAGER'S OFFICE.

THE USHER PROBABLY RECOGNIZED US FROM THE EARLIER "JEDI" SHOW
MIKE STONE'S HAIR ISN'T EXACTLY INCONSPICUOUS
HONEST, SIR! WE DIDN'T SNEAK IN!
"ONCE YOU START DOWN THE DARK PATH, FOREVER WILL IT DOMINATE YOUR DESTINY."

I'M SURE A LOT OF KIDS TRIED SNEAKING IN AND STUFF
LOOK AT THIS HAIR! LOOK AT THIS SHIRT! DO YOU THINK I **NEED** TO BE SNEAKING INTO MOVIES?
I CAN AFFORD THE PRICE OF A TICKET, SHANK YOU VERY MUCH!
"YOU'RE A FEISTY LITTLE ONE, BUT YOU'LL SOON LEARN SOME RESPECT."

BUT WE WOULD **NEVER** SNEAK IN TO SEE "JEDI"
WE ALWAYS PAID FOR THAT ONE. IT WAS WORTH IT
"SUPERMAN 3"... WELL, THAT WAS ANOTHER STORY
COME ON! THEY HAVE TO BE IN ONE OF THOSE POCKETS! YOU AND YOUR STUPID CARGO PANTS!

THEY... MUST... BE... HERE... SOMEWHERE...
I DON'T RECALL EXACTLY HOW IT ALL WENT DOWN, BUT I REMEMBER THE MANAGER GIVING US A PRETTY CHEESY LECTURE ON HOW SNEAKING IN WAS LIKE STEALING AND HOW IT WOULD ONLY LEAD US TO BIGGER CRIMES ONE DAY

MIKE NEVER FOUND THE TICKETS, SO WE WERE ASKED TO LEAVE. BUT WE WERE LIKE THE REBEL ALLIANCE AND COULDN'T BE DETERRED THAT EASILY...
THIS SUCKS EGGS!
WAIT, WAIT, WAIT. WE'RE NOT GOING TO SEE THE SAME MOVIE AGAIN!
YEAH, WE DIDN'T EVEN GET TO FINISH IT THIS TIME.
BUT IT STILL COUNTS, JAMIE. MAKE SURE TO ADD IT TO THE COUNT!
LOOK, IT'S A GREAT FLICK, BUT CAN'T WE SEE SOMETHING DIFFERENT? IS THIS WHAT WE'RE GOING TO DO OUR ENTIRE SUMMER VACATION?
UM... SO, WOULD YOU RATHER MESS UP YOUR HAIR BY GOING SWIMMING OR PLAYING BASEBALL?
"WHAT ABOUT "PORKY'S 2"? IT'S PLAYING DOWN THE STREET...
BUT WE'VE SEEN THAT **TWICE** ALREADY!
OKAY, HOW ABOUT "RISKY BUSINESS"? OR EVEN "TRADING PLACES"?
YOU JUST WANNA SEE THOSE AGAIN 'CAUSE OF ALL THE NAKED CHICKS!
WELL, **DOY**!
REBECCA DEMORNAY.
JAMIE LEE CURTIS.
SIGH
BUY YOUR TICKET ALREADY, AND HANG ONTO IT YOURSELF THIS TIME.
FINE! AT LEAST PRINCESS LEIA SHOWS SOME SKIN...
SOMEONE LEND ME MONEY, THOUGH. I'M ALL OUT EXCEPT FOR BUS FARE.
"THE MIGHTY JABBA ASKS WHY HE MUST PAY 50 THOUSAND."
"JABBA OFFERS THE SUM OF 36, AND I DO SUGGEST YOU TAKE IT."
YOU GUYS ARE SUCH GEEKS...

THE COPYBOOK TALES
"As Good As It Gets"
by J. Torres & Tim Levins
MARK HA
CARRIE F
HARRISO
JEDI
WHAT A GREAT SUMMER THAT WAS
WE FIGURED OUT A SHORTCUT THROUGH THE MALL FROM THE SUBWAY STATION TO THE IMPERIAL WHERE "JEDI" WAS PLAYING, AND WE THOUGHT WE WERE SO CLEVER
AND WE FOUND ABOUT THREE GAFFS IN THE MOVIE WE WERE SURE NO ONE ELSE IN THE WORLD NOTICED
BUT PROBABLY THE SMARTEST THING WE LEARNED THAT SUMMER WAS TO NEVER LET MIKE BROWN HANG ON TO OUR TICKETS
IF MOM ONLY KNEW THE "TROUBLE" I WAS GETTING INTO IN "DANGEROUS" DOWNTOWN MONTREAL...
"IT IS POINTLESS TO RESIST, MY SON."
CAREFUL, JAMIE!
IT'S ALL FUN AND GAMES UNTIL SOMEONE LOSES AN EYE...
SO, YOU GUYS REALLY THINK WE CAN SEE "JEDI" 100 TIMES BEFORE WE GO BACK TO SCHOOL...?
FOR
RETUR
JE
DESPITE A NEW "STAR WARS" MOVIE IN THEATRES, AND EVEN WITH CARGO PANTS MAKING A COMEBACK, I DOUBT IT'LL EVER BE AS GOOD AS IT WAS IN 1983...

Rich Henn & Club 408 Graphics presents

Hershal the Rat™ in ...

MEMORIUM

Sparky the Moose

Hershal the Rat

WE ARE HERE TO REMEMBER OUR DEAR FRIEND, *MISS CLUCK*.

Johnny On-The-Spot

Johnny Wet-Spot

Rip the Human

I'M WITH STUPID

WHAT A *HOTTIE*.

SHE MOST CERTAINLY WAS.

Marvin Muffin Mixel

I THINK THE TWINS OVER THERE, PROBABLY KNEW HER BEST, THOUGH.
...BURP...!
YO, JOHNNIES!
YOU TWO NUMBNUTS WANNA CONTRIBUTE, OR AM I JUST YANKING MY OWN CRANK OVER HERE?

WELL, I THINK MY BROTHER WAS ACTUALLY CLOSER TO MISS CLUCK THAN I WAS.

YOU KNOW I FIND THAT A LITTLE HARD TO BELIEVE.

IT'S TRUE. WET-SPOT WOULD GO OFF BEHIND THE BARN WITH HER, SOMETIMES FOR HOURS...
OURS WAS A FORBIDDEN LOVE.

JOHNNY... THERE'S ABSOLUTELY NO NEED TO FEEL ASHAMED.
I'M PRETTY SURE WHAT THE TWO OF YOU HAD WAS A BEAUTIFUL THING.

THAT'S EASY FOR YOU TO SAY. I HAD TO WATCH THE WHOLE THING.
WELL, ACTUALLY... I WAS JUST TAKING NOTES.
I'M WITH STUPID

SHE COULD'VE PUT ALL HER EGGS IN MY BASKET.

WELL THEN... LET'S HOIST OUR BEER CANS TO ONE BEAUTIFUL BIRD.

TO MISS CLUCK !

ALLRIGHT, ENOUGH OF THE SENTIMENTAL CHIT-CHAT.
I'M HUNGRY. *WHITE MEAT* OR *DARK?*

I'M A LEG MAN!

I'M A *BREAST MAN*, MYSELF
YOU *WOULD* NOW PASS VASELINE HAND ME BEER.
FIN

Magic Inkwell
comic strip theatre
A shimmer in the desert air
Allude to things not really there
Barren land of life stripped bare
Except these gentle dreams...
Z
Now from silence comes to be
Filled with rhyme and harmony
A melancholy melody
Nothing's what it seems...
cayetano

Gentle twilight fantasy
Carried on dry, arid breeze
Silver dewdrop notes now leave
In midair to gleam

POP!

Creation in its purest form
From nothingness, something is born
To greet the brightest desert morn
And stir us all from dream

You

can't

ignore

or tame

the muse

It's

inspiration

put

to

use

Before, like caged birds once set loose,

Quickly

fly

away

fin.

here, kitty!
SIS

FROSTY

the feline ice queen

whitey.
DAD

FROSTY WAS MY SISTER'S CAT AND SHE DIDN'T ***LIKE*** ME MUCH. THAT'S PROBABLY BECAUSE I WAS LOUD, ***OBNOXIOUS*** AND DESTRUCTIVE. I HAD A 6-YEAR-OLD'S "SCIENTIFIC" INTEREST IN BURNING THINGS AND DROPPING ***LARGE ROCKS*** ON MY TOYS.

ONLY ONCE DID FROSTY DEIGN TO PLAY WITH ME. IT WAS A SUNDAY I'M ***SURE***, ON ONE OF THOSE DREARY WEEK-ENDS WHEN I WAS ALONE WITH ***DAD***.

HE PACED HIMSELF THROUGH A ***TWELVE-PACK*** AND THE LAST OF HIS STASH, WHILE JUGGLING THE ***TV CHANNELS***: COLLEGE FOOTBALL, TENNIS AND ***GODZILLA*** *VS. THAT TURTLE-THING.*

MY SMEAR OF LEGOS ON THE CARPET FLOOR ***INTRIGUED*** FROSTY. SHE SWATTED AT PIECES ***ANIMATED*** BY MY HAND PASSING THROUGH THE PILE.

RECOGNIZING A RARE OPPORTUNITY, I TIED SOME STRING TO A ***GLOB OF LEGOS*** AND BAITED HER INTO THE FRONT YARD WHERE IT HAD BEGUN TO RAIN.

WILD-EYED, IGNORING THE WETNESS AND HER ***REPUTATION,*** FROSTY POUNCED AFTER THE TUMBLING ***CHUNK*** BEHIND ME.

IT WAS ***HOT AND HUMID*** FOR CALIFORNIA. THE WARM DROPS FELT UNNATURAL, BUT SOME-HOW AGREED WITH THE CAT'S ***WEIRD*** MOOD.

WHEN THE SKY ***RE-OPENED,*** THE RAIN DRIZZLED AWAY AND SHE LOST INTEREST, ***SKULKING*** OFF TO PREEN HERSELF.

KNOWING IT WAS THE END OF OUR AFFAIR, I WANDERED BACK INTO THE HOUSE AND WATCHED *GODZILLA'S* ULTIMATE TRIUMPH BY KNOCKING THE ***TURTLE-CREATURE*** ON HIS BACK, NEVER TO ARIGHT HIMSELF.

WE DON'T KNOW WHO FIRST NOTICED SUNSPOTS.

IN 28 B.C., ASTRONOMERS IN CHINA RECORDED SMALL, CHANGING DARK PATCHES ON THE SUN'S SURFACE. SOME GREEK TEXTS FROM THE FOURTH CENTURY B.C. ALSO MAKE REFERENCE TO THE MYSTERIOUS MARKS WHICH PEBBLE THE SUN'S SURFACE.

BY THE END OF THE 20TH CENTURY, SCIENTISTS LOOKING TO WRITE ONE MORE PAPER EXPLAINING AWAY THE MYSTERIES OF THE UNIVERSE REDUCED SUNSPOTS TO "DARK AREAS THAT ARE COOLER THAN THEIR SURROUNDINGS BECAUSE OF STRONG MAGNETIC FIELDS WHICH FORM BELOW THE SUN'S SURFACE."

VERY PRACTICAL. NO WONDER EVERYONE WAS SO DEPRESSED BACK THEN.

BRIGHT SPOTS

an ASTOUNDING SPACE THRILLS short story by STEVE CONLE

www.astoundingspacethrills.co

THEREMIN, ISN'T IT FANTASTIC?

I GUESS.

YOU *GUESS?* THE FIRST TWO EARTHLINGS TO SAUNTER ACROSS THE SUN'S SURFACE AND YOU SAY, "I GUESS?"

SHEESH, WHY SO GLUM, CHUM?

I DON'T KNOW, ARGOSY.
ALL THE NEGATIVITY AND ANGER!
SAYING, "NOTHING'S AS GOOD AS IT ONCE WAS."
I'M ALMOST STARTING TO BELIEVE IT.

NOT THAT I AGREE WITH THEM, BUT LOOK AT IT THIS WAY, DOESN'T THAT MAKE *RIGHT NOW* AS GOOD AS IT WILL EVER BE.
AND THANKFULLY, WE'RE ALSO AS YOUNG AS WE'LL EVER BE, TOO!
I'D HATE TO THINK THAT THE BEST DAYS ARE AHEAD AND WE WON'T BE AROUND TO SEE 'EM.

HIS WILL PICK YOU UP!

IT'S WHY I BROUGHT YOU HERE IN SPITE OF YOUR MOOD.

SUNSPOTS?

YOU DRAGGED ME TO THE BRIGHTEST SPOT IN THE SOLAR SYSTEM TO SEE THE DARKEST?

TO SEE THEM ***BOTH***. THEY'RE NOT MUTUALLY EXCLUSIVE, IT JUST DEPENDS ON WHICH ONE YOU'RE FOCUSING ON.

AND IF YOU JUST LOOK A LITTLE CLOSER, EVEN THE DARKEST SPOTS HOLD WONDERS YOU NEVER EXPECTED.

STOUNDING SPACE THRILLS IS PUBLISHED BY DAY ONE COMICS
O. BOX 12192 ARLINGTON, VA 22219
TP://ASTOUNDINGSPACETHRILLS.COM EMAIL: STEVE@STEVECONLEY.COM

WANT FRIES WITH THAT?

Comic Creator's Day Jobs

SPX99

C.K. Lichenstein II

If you're like me, you've always wondered if one can really make a living doing comics day in and day out. Sure, people like Alan Moore aren't going to be hurting anytime soon (especially after selling the rights to From Hell) but what about those talented underdogs of the alternative comics world? With that in mind, I eagerly sought the truth of how different creators supported themselves as they sacrificed all for their art.

To be fair, I'll go first. Like many I don't make enough off of my writing to survive so I have to have a regular job. For several years now it has been Graphic Design and, until recently, I had been at one dental equipment company creating all of their literature, from catalogs to manuals. It was terribly dry design work so, when I could, I often did other work including laying out a mini-comic, writing articles and comic stories and... well, playing video games (though not often). The biggest problem I had was that people walked behind me all day and my computer screen was COMPLETELY visible. I became very adept at sensing when people were approaching and quickly switched back to a work screen. I'm amazed I never got caught.

Box Office Poison features a myriad of diverse and fascinating characters that have honestly grown and moved forward since the first issue and just keeps getting better. Their creator, Alex Robinson, has toiled at several jobs but his best day job was at Barnes & Noble. "I worked there for seven years(!) while I was going to school and then when I started doing BOP mini-comics," Robinson told me. "I finally quit in 1997, under the delusion that I could draw full time. Since then I've worked a couple of odd jobs (word processing, ushering) but none has influenced my work the way the bookstore did." One of BOP's main characters is Sherman, who works at a bookstore and is constantly dealing with inane questions from customers all day long. "At first it was a great vent for the hatred I had for the place, but since quitting, I've had a harder time writing books tore issues because I don't feel nearly as passionate about stupid customers. Naturally, people tell me they LOVE the bookstore stories." (http://members.aol.com/bopalex/index.html)

When Gene Yang's Gordon Yamamoto and the King of the Geeks was released, one could immediately sense Yang had a good sense of the caste system of teens. Sure, some of it has to do with once being a te himself, but I think his day job helps a bit. "During t day," said Yang, "I teach Computer Science at Bish O'Dowd High School, a Catholic high school in Oaklar California. Since all of my projects so far have involv high school kids, I think that my job strongly influenc my comic." When asked what his students think of l other job he said, "Most of 'em think it's pretty cool; sor of 'em are pestering me to put them into my comic. haven't yet because if I were to in a truthful mann they'd be pissed." Look for his new self-published bo Loyola Chin and the San Peligran Order, which is "a s of continuation of GyatKotG" and Duncan's Kingd with art by Derek Kirk (Cell) from Image. (http://www.s ius.com/~geneyang/)

Chynna Clugston-Major's hilarious Bl Monday (appearing in Dark Horse Presents, Action G and Oni Double Feature) is based on some of her frien which makes me almost scared to meet them. Now a f time student, she recently worked at a B. Dalt Bookstore. Chynna shocked me by saying, "I fucki hated helping the public! I never met more illiterate p ple anywhere than in a bookstore, which completely b fled me. What annoyed me more was that the majority these people that looked over and saw comic books n the counter had the audacity to insult people who re them, when they can't even fucking read anything wi out pictures anyway!" For the most part, this cyni attitude doesn't really make it to her own pages, l every once in a while it does slip in. "For the most pa grew an even bigger distaste for the general pub They're sometimes rather anti-inspiration (http://www.geocities.com/Tokyo/Dojo/8206/index.ht

Speaking of cynical brings to mind Jim l and his devastatingly funny Caffeine. He told me that is a delivery guy for a large national copy shop "t shall remain nameless." Having plenty of free time yo think he'd be using it to draw comics but instead he u it more creatively. "Sometimes I find myself jett around killing time," he honestly confessed. "I so times go home and work on my comics, but not as of as I should. One time I saw a movie in the theater on clock. It was the X-Files movie and I'm glad I saw it on company time because it wasn't that great. I figured time I was watching the movie I made the money I sp n the flick back and then some. I couldn't totally enjoy t though. I was kind of nervous about it and my pager ept going off. How dare they expect me to work!" He oes get all the free copying he wants which sure does ome in handy for him and his friends. (http://www.slave-abor.com/)

James Kochalka's offbeat and bittersweet omics are many and varied but two of his best are Magic oy and the Word of God and Paradise Sucks. For the last ix years Kochalka had been a waiter at a Chinese restau-ant called The Peking Duck House." Towards the end all ny comics were being written between running around erving my tables. I would take the orders on these little ocket-sized pads of paper, and I would draw rough drafts f my graphic novels as thumbnail sketches." That must ave been a sight to behold. Recently he quit waiting ables to draw and create music full time. " It seems npossible but I've been making a living on my 'art.' My ear was that without the stimulation of my job my mind night atrophy, but I'm getting into the swing of things, nd I feel I'm making big creative strides. I plan to be job ee for at least one year, but hopefully forever. It's cer-ainly not impossible to create art while slaving away at job, but what a wonderful luxury to not have to!" ttp://www.indyworld.com/kochalka/)

When one thinks of alternative comics, one ame has to be near the top of the list, Matt Feazell - king f the mini-comics. Back in the 80's Feazell was a used ecord store clerk." During the week," he told me, " I was e only one running the shop during the day and traffic as often slow so I ended up spending a lot of time just lis-ning to loud music and drawing comics. How cool is at?" Not only did he listen to bands like The Clash, The amones, Sex Pistols, and Elvis Costello, but he was able get turned onto different styles, like Cajun music, and eate mini-comics like Cynicalman. Nowadays Feazell is eading my day job turf with his own studio doing web esign/production. " I also help out on a monthly maga-ne at their offices about 30 hours over one weekend the d of every month." I'm dying to see what his ads look ke, but I guess it would be asking too much to have Anti-ocialman pushing products. ttp://www.wraithspace.com/cynicalman/index.html)

Brian Bigg's Dear Julia made such a strong npact on me that I immediately sought out his ederick & Eloise one shot; you should do the same. ggs says his illustrating at home job " could be con-rued a 55555lquote day-job,' although I am sure that ose poor bastards who have to get up in the morning d drive somewhere and do whatever menial stupid task eir boss says and eat lunch in half an hour and drive me pissed and experience road rage and then yell at eir girlf riend and go to sleep angry and confused and ddened by the whole experience may disagree with me." The lucky artist sleeps in, watches TV, takes long lunches and draws pictures for magazines and agencies. "Back when I had a job (see description above) I used to write comics in meetings. When I quit my job no one was surprised. I think they wondered why I was there as long as I was." (http://www.MrBiggs.com/index.html)

Growing up in Houston, Texas, Scott Gilbert's True Artist Tales weekly strips were a must read and many were collected in It's All True: The Best of True Artist Tales. Though Gilbert makes plenty of bread doing commercial art and web graphics, he still retains his day job at the Circulation Desk at the Rice University Library. " I am a humble clerk," Gilbert confided in me, "checking books in and out, billing folks for lost items, and generally helping the mentally handicapped that make up the majority of our patron base." Besides some web research, he rarely does any comics at work but does "all of my critical writing on comics (for the Comics Journal and Submedia Magazine) up here. I am writing these words at the Circ desk right now!" Of course, having to deal with so many people, some true-life incidents have made there way into Gilbert's strips. Sharing the agony must be good for the soul. (http://www.apeshot.com/)

Ian Smith writes the hilarious Oddjob from Slave Labor, which is lusciously illustrated by his brother Ty. Ty pays most of his bills with freelance art (check out BadAzz Mofo) and as an "illustrator/sometime designer for The Math Learning Center, a math book publisher." Ian told me that he works "as an Information Processor for an evil market research firm that is employed by Microsoft to make up numbers for use in their anti-trust case. I am possibly the lowest paid computer programmer on the face of the earth!" Besides having to inform the masses that New Mexico is a state and not a country, he does get in some important comic writing time. "I secretly record the antics of only the stupidest of my co-workers, which I then recycle into my comic. I also try and steal as much time as I can plotting out Oddjob when no one's looking." More power to you brother! (http://www.teleport.com/ ~ megalon/)

I was surprised at how many creators were earning a lot, if not all, of their main dough through freelance illustrations, especially with all the troubles in this field... but then, their money wasn't coming from comics. With the web being such a large asset, many of these creators have found new outlets for their craft, and thus new work. I recommend seeking out those sites and wasting as much time as possible. One final note: when I asked Marc Hempel (Mars, Gregory, Tug and Buster) what his day job was he left me with these stunning answers. " Comics, unfortunately, are my day job, and on rare occasions I actually work on comics while I'm at work!" Okay, he also does a lot of freelance art but you gotta love that answer.

ICAF EXPERIENCE

SPX99

In September 1998, Igo Prassel and Jacob Klemencic were invited to participate in the ICAF/SPX event in Bethesda, Maryland. Once over the pond, the two ambassadors of Eastern European comics decided to see some more of northestern US as well as some of Canada.A lot of things happened - the ones delineated below are some of the PG-rated ones...

Washington Dulles Airport: after being neatly categorized and put in lines according to nationality, it's time to meet His Majesty the Immigration Officer. As not so long ago, the States decided that the citizens of that tidy, hard working, prosperous and unkniwn little country on the

sunny side of the Alps didn't need a visa to visit the land of opportunity, we expected extensive verbal wars against ignorance. But no such luck: as soon as His Majesty hears that one of us is an art historian, our entry suddenly depends on a sole question, "In what year did Michelangelo decorate the Sistine Chapel?"

Six years of hard study - not to mention all the excursions across Italy - did pay off. We were admitted into the USA!

First Morning in Bethesda. the alar clock is set for 8:00 a.m.

Good Morning America!

After three comic-filled days and tv booze etc.-filled nights (not to mention the jetlag sight grows dim and thoughts get fuzzy... As we p down our bags filled with comics, posters, e swapped for Stripburgers to clean up "The Mo european Dealer's Table in the History of America Alternatice Comics" a tragedy happened. Instead much needed and deserved rest, a quest for lost tre sures began! Even with a member of the organizi committee and a Dutch colleague involved, it looked rather hopeless until... Igor mustered up his charm, determination and knowledge Spanish, stepped to the cleaners and askes wheth "Usted sabes donde este el material que vosotr habes limpado?" Manuel's dirty finger pointed o a location. Yes! After some digging, the treasure was unearthed. "Gracias, Manuel!" The celebration can start!

Strolling casually through the streats f Montreal, we stumble upon a museum devoted to ›cal history. As it was our first day in Canada, we ›cided to get acquainted with the local spirit and ent in. All the seriousness that was necessary at e ticket counter in order to get the free tickets at journalists are entitled to was lost the moment ır eyes behend a hockey version of "table soccer"

pee! The game could go on for ours if the musen guard hadn't looked so cross.

Back to the States: the Customs Officer as surprised at the amount of funnybooks import- into the Land of the Free. We were lucky again – he happened to find copies of Jakob's "Dandruff" ini, he'd probably take it as a personal insult and ›'d be in deep trouble.

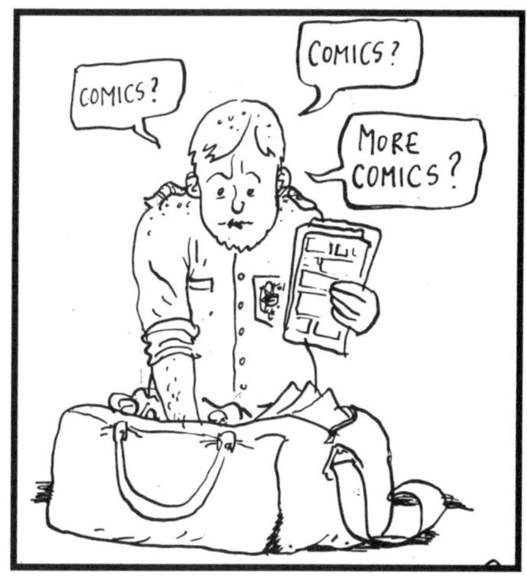

The most fascinating comic shop experience: during a Sunday afternoon signing that we had, the best comic shop in New England was suddenly flooded b not-so-young ladies with just one word on their lips, "Superman." It was time to fly anyway.

CBLDF AND THE EXPO

Creating Space for Diversity

SPX99

Chris Oarr

The book you' re holding in your hands was produced for two simple reasons. First and foremost, THE EXPO99 Comic serves as a showcase for a diverse array of comics talent. But this book is also designed to raise money for the Comic Book Legal Defense Fund, a non-profit organization protecting the First Amendment rights of the comics community. These two purposes are, in fact, more closely allied than you might think.

The CBLDF's guiding principle is that comics deserve the same freedom of expression accorded film, literature, and other media. While ostensibly guaranteed by the First Amendment, the right to free speech is constantly under assault from over-zealous police officers, grandstanding politicians and conservative religious groups. Comics, popular music, and photography, as new art forms with uniquely expressive powers, bear the brunt of these attacks. But no artistic media is truly safe in America's on-going culture wars, and the right to free expression must be vigorously defended in our nation' s courts.

That defense, of course, costs huge sums of money, money that the average comic retailer or artist simply doesn' t have. Since its inception in 1986, the CBLDF has coordinated and funded the legal defense of dozens of comics creators and retailers in cases involving parody, obscenity, free access, and more. A single court case can cost upwards of $70,000 in legal bills. The Fund can only exist and operate thanks to the generous donations and support of comics fans and professionals who love the medium and care about its future.

Which is what the Fund is really all about. By protecting free expression in comics, the CBLDF helps insure that this still young medium will continue to grow and develop, that it remains a capable vehicle for art, for invention, for diversity. The Fund's mission is driven by innovative, avant-garde work, by those creators out there exploring the unique possibilities of comics, and those retailers and publishers who are supportive of such work. Together, w can create a space for comics to thrive and experimer and flourish, whether that space is on the Internet, i more stores, on more shelves, or in more hands.

The organizers of THE EXPO have realize all this from the beginning. Both THE EXPO99 Comi and THE EXPO itself celebrate the enormous diversit and potential of the medium. Witness the huge democr cy of styles and voices in this book alone. And THE EXP has always been willing to put its money where its mout is, to invest in the future of comics with an annual eve and comic expressly designed to benefit the Fund.

That means the 100% of the proceeds fro this book go to the CBLDF. This is all the more impressiv considering that the artists, writers, and designers a contributed their work pro bono.

Proceeds from THE EXPO al support the Fund. In fact, THE EXI was the CBLDF' s third highest fund-ra ing event last year. That's quite a achievement, considering the number larger shows the Fund attends. Over t years, this small show, a gathering those devoted to what is traditional the least profitable portion of the indu try, has raised more than $15,000 help protect free speech for everyone comics.

How can you help? Buying copy of THE EXPO99 Comic is a go start. Read artists doing innovati work, and buy their books at com shops that understand the need to sto all kinds of comics. Come out for T EXPO, and other comic conventio across the country.

Even better, you can help dire ly by becoming a card-carrying Meml of the CBLDF. The annual dues are or $25, and your contribution goes straight to the Fund War Chest for future cases. You'll get access to spec Members-Only events at cons across the country, as w as a nifty Membership Card. Not to mention the peace mind that comes from investing in the future of sor thing you love.

For more information about the Fund and becoming a Member, visit the CBLDF web-site at http://www.cbldf.org. You can also sign up for a free subscription to Busted the Fund' s quarterly newsletter which features case updates, con reports, upcoming events, and more. Or call the Fund directly at 1-800-99-CBLDF. Your support is crucial in preserving the art of comics into the next millennium.